The Ledge

A Novel

RICHARD CURTIS HAUSCHILD

First published by Dog Ear Publishing
4010 W. 86th Street, Ste H
Indianapolis, IN 46268
www.dogearpublishing.net

ISBN: 978-160844-133-4

This book is printed on acid-free paper.

Printed in the United States of America

CHAPTER ONE

I never got up early to write, but to see the stars and to walk Sorry. That dog came along at the time in my life when I was afraid of being in bed too long. The ghosts of regret at the end of my bed made me rise up early. It worked out good for her, me being afraid. Sorry had sheep in her blood and wanted to be out there on the perimeter where she could keep an eye on their shadows in her mind. I bowed to her compulsions. I had failure in my blood and rued it. In January, the morning sky before the sunrise had a hint of the Spring constellations, a weak promise, but a sincere one. I let Sorry lead me into that promised land. The snow would crunch under a boot and paw at that hour. And so I learned that I felt the safest place in life was out crunching January snow in the predawn with Castor, Pollux, and Sorry.

Roland Heinz stood in the snow beneath the tower and wings of the huge white wind turbine and listened to its throb. He was both amazed by its power and sorry that he had allowed it on his property. It was a daily regret. Like growing old. He stared up at the whirling blades and tried not to see them as clock hands gone crazy. At sixty-nine years old, he was resolved to be bent by time, but he didn't want to have to bow to it. He knew it was passing quickly now and he wanted to savor the calendar like a good book, not watch it making someone else's electricity.

Today was Friday in tiny Pipe, Wisconsin, a grocery and haircut day and he never really enjoyed the time invested in doing either chore. Especially the damned haircut, but he knew it was overdue and he had very special guests arriving over the weekend. He wasn't vain, but neither did he want to put anyone off with his disheveled appearance. Nothing worse than a messy old man.

The heater on his Nissan pickup was efficient even though the dashboard thermometer showed -8 degrees. With the morning sun at his back he rumbled down his long driveway to Highway 151, turned left and headed into Fond du Lac, the nearest big town. A myriad of ice shanties dotted the white surface of Lake Winnebago, but he doubted there were many fishermen dangling lures in these temps. Then again, he mused that brandy was a mighty antifreeze.

The barbershop, an out-of-date term in Roland's mind was really mostly an old woman's blueing parlor with a tanning bed in the back. It was at least out on the city edge, which made actually driving into town unnecessary. At his age, he found his tolerance for the increasing traffic around Fond du Lac had reached its limit. What once had been a farm supply and railroad town was now a bedroom community for Milwaukee and its northern suburbs. Change and the required adaptation moved in opposite directions for Roland Heinz.

Roland Heinz was a large and still handsome man even if he had lost an inch or two of his former six foot three height to the sixties sag. Stomach problems had kept him trim in its agonizing way. His hair, which had once been blonde, was now not exactly gray, but more the color of spoiled butter mixed with pewter at the temples. He was proud, in a modest way, that he had not lost it and it grew fast above his high brow and large ears. His eyes were stone gray as though they had been quarried from the local limestone. Even when a smile flickered across his lips, his eyes were slower to ignite. His nose, like many a senor in these parts, told an old drinking story.

The young girl who would cut his hair introduced herself as Becca and shook his hand as she led him to the chair. She was a pretty girl, he thought, and probably never more so than when sharing the mirror with his grim visage. However, like most men past their rutting prime, he always felt the presence of who he was at twenty-five deep inside him. That presence often ignored present day and wanted to flirt. He almost cooed as she touched his head. She had a faint scent of citrus on her fingers.

"So what are you up to today?" Becca asked.

"About six-two," replied Roland, the reply going over her head like a tracer bullet.

"Huh, oh yeah." When you don't know what someone is talking about agree with them. It was part of the hair cutting training, he supposed.

"So you have the day off?" More small talk as spoiled butter pooled in his lap.

"I have every day off."

"So you're like retired, huh?"

Roland saw this leading to a useless conversation and headed it off at the pass. The twenty-five year old was already gone with the word 'retired.'

"You could say that. Cold day out there." Weather was safe.

"So what did you do before?" She was mindlessly, unintentionally dogging him.

"I was a quarry worker for many years and now I am a writer."

"A writer. Wow! What do you write?"

He knew where this was heading and went for the short answer.

"Books."

"Oh, yeah, I read one once."

Roland looked at her pretty face in the mirror. She was combing his hair into neat rows and snipping them off a half inch at a time. He wondered what the one book was that she read once, but his mind was telling him she hadn't finished it whatever it was. He knew he was being a silent snob and almost smiled. Once again she picked up the thread.

"So what *have* you written?"

It was time to launch another tracer bullet. "I've only written two books that were of any note. One was titled, *A Winter Light* and the other was *The Tap Root*. I doubt you ever heard of them." He had just listed the titles of two Pulitzer Prize winners for fiction. It was not a revelation that had any chance of inflating him here. In other cities and other circles he was a literary god.

"No. They in a store?"

Becca had finished the cut and was brushing off the sheet.

"Yes, you could find them I suppose."

"Kewl." She removed the neck clip and whipped off the sheet with a flourish. "There, all done."

Yes, she was done, he thought. Cute girl, bad haircut. He had taken note that she had not even inquired what his name was. An author was anonymous in these parts. Unless, you were a ghost-writer for a Green Bay Packer. He paid and tipped her well and headed next door to the Piggly Wiggly to get some supplies. As he shopped everything he touched seemed 'kewl.' He was already itching from the hairs on his neck and couldn't wait to get home to Ghost Farm to wash off the morning.

Early on Roland Heinz was aware that local folks had begun calling his place a ghost farm. It was one of those spreads that when sold by the last generation of family farmers had ceased to be a working farm and had become dormant estate. So it inevitably became Ghost Farm with the spirits of dairy cows and chickens to haunt it properly. As near as Roland could tell the farm house had been built around 1900; an eight room, two story popular plan of its day. The barn was probably built in the forties and stood out for its light yellow paint job instead of the usual red. The out buildings were made of cement blocks with those opaque glass block windows, popular after WWII. The workshop, which was probably originally a cheese house, served as his writing studio. He had adopted it as such because of the many windows. The exposure to daylight was the trigger for his creativity. Emulating certain paint artists, everything began and ended for Roland Heinz with light.

It was not just the light that stimulated Roland, but also the view. Ghost Farm sat high on the Niagara Escarpment, better known locally as The Ledge. The view to the west took in the vast expanse of Lake Winnebago and the distant shores of Oshkosh and other lakeshore communities. The

The Ledge

Ledge was an immense slab of limestone and granite that circled over the top of the Great Lakes, eventually cut by the Niagara Falls to the east. Here in east central Wisconsin it provided a wall of rock that supported several quarries that had employed a younger Roland, but it was prized mostly now as real estate. Height meant view, view meant value.

In a recent manifestation of that high ground, some of the properties upon The Ledge became wind farms, home base to huge white turbines rising into the sky. Roland had sold a lease to Alliant Energy, when a far corner of his lot was sited for the final windmill in a string of twenty that cut across the land from Silica, standing like an alien army phalanx. He was seduced by the idea of green energy, but realized he had made a mistake when the landscape became so drastically changed by the behemoths. It was a stupid mistake, but he was loath to admit it; especially to the woman who owned the land behind his place. Heinz and his neighbor, Meg Bollander already had a history before the turbine issue. Many years had clouded their issues and blurred some ancient hurts, but pain, like a moving object, tends to stay in motion once it has been set in motion. Like the turbines.

Roland had witnessed Meg glowering at the tower as it was erected the year before. She rode her red ATV out to the fence line last fall and stood up with hands on hips, her aura of rage bright and dark at the same time. On more than one occasion he had tried to speak to her, but she saw him first and drove off abruptly. He recalled wistfully what a time they once had in her cornfield when they were young. He knew that was the heart of their problem. But, that field was now just a stubbled old battleground of corn whiskers sticking up through the snow. The turbine, blades turned into the northeast wind, hummed indifferently to past or present times. They killed the birds, scared the cows, and paid for new tractors. The future was always going to be tricky.

CHAPTER TWO

I got on well with women early in my life. I was tall and forward, which helped mightily. And yet, I know I feared them as well. Their power over us men. I heard many grown men call out for their mothers and wives while under fire in Viet Nam. Guys wept for their womenfolk. Soldiers only stopped drugging long enough to write a love letter home. Whispering, screaming Mother Mary's name was as common to a wounded man as bleeding. Saigon hookers and bar singers were worshiped, too. Anything female. Anything softer than metal. The salvation of sex. Women marched beside us in our minds. All of them. The voices in our dreams. I held Karin's hand in the jungle. She was my waiting woman, the floating face of a heart. I recognized that as love even when I was lost in the world. Karin's face. What I wouldn't give to see it again. She was the rib closest to my heart. She protected it and now that protection is gone. How do you replace a rib in your chest?

Molly Costello was nursing a tepid mug of coffee at her desk and surfing the web for flights out of Boston to Chicago or Milwaukee. The magazine used to have people to book flights and hotels, but they were laid off a couple years ago. It didn't really matter. Her fingers flew over the keyboard in delight. She had landed the Pulitzer interview and she was the envy of everyone on the staff. A few of her coworkers who were in the office on this Saturday morning wandered by for congratulations, complexions greened by envy. It was the happiest day of Molly's life in those first few hours of glory basking. The years of snappy reviews born of dedicated research had paid their dividends. Getting the Roland Heinz interview was her own lesser Pulitzer. To actually meet the recluse writer was a coup in itself. As far as anyone knew, he had never granted an interview.

Heinz wrote; didn't talk much, but Molly would finally be the ear. Her morning mind was racing far ahead of her fingers. Hard covers and paperback editions of his two most famous books sat on her desk.

"Molly!" It was Erin More, the senior writer at *Art Harvest* magazine; she being the one seemingly passed over by the editor, Harry Stompe. Molly turned to her name with an invisible shield activated. No one would diminish her today. Not even Erin. And it was not necessarily a good sign that she was smiling.

"Oh, hi, Erin. I guess you heard."

"I heard, I did and congratulations."

Molly quickly examined the possibilities of how to proceed. Erin beat her to it.

"He requested you, you know." Erin tossed out, still smiling mysteriously.

"I'm sorry...?"

"Roland Heinz asked for you. He requested you to come see him."

"No shit?" This had taken Molly by surprise. Harry had not mentioned the request part and it threw her. It was instantly as though the personal request had trumped her writing and interviewing skills. The information somehow conflicted her.

"Typical of Harry not giving out the details," Erin continued. "I didn't even know you knew Roland Heinz."

"I don't, Erin. Never met or even talked to the man. Never exchanged so much as an email. Are you sure that is why I got the assignment?"

Erin stared now with the smile frozen. A laundry list of possible replies, conjectures, and quips scrolled across her inner screen. A mystery had emerged. It was something she loved and hated. "I assumed..." The word was posed and drawn out.

"I know," said Molly, "you assumed I knew the guy or you would have landed the job. Hey, I assumed you would get it, too. I have no idea how this happened, but I am not put off by it. I am intrigued, I must admit, but..." How to continue the conversation from here was clouded. Erin had lost the excuse

7

for her being passed over. Now the pain was clear on her face, although somehow the smile remained. Time to end this, thought Molly.

"I had better go talk to Harry," Molly mumbled and then focused on Erin. "Hey, listen we'll talk later, okay? I'm as dazed as you are right now. When I get the answers I'll buzz you."

Erin nodded and did a cute about face, walking a way with just the slightest head shake. Molly picked up the phone on her desk and dialed Harry Stompe's office.

Molly Costello was one of those women of whom people would always make the distinction between pretty and beautiful, she being closer to the pretty end of the scale. This was not a bad thing, but she always wondered why the beautiful part had to be left off. She knew how she looked. She beheld herself often enough. But now that she neared mid-forty she regarded herself with a closer appraisal. The mahogany blonde hair now had some gray woven in. The green eyes were framed by life lines. As was the wide smile. She kept her figure gym trim without the muscles because she was somewhat short and stayed away from adding chunky to not being beautiful.

Molly was single, never married although she had two adopted daughters. Melanie was twelve and Vietnamese and Sonia was seven and from the refugee camps in Sudan. The family was Catholic, Buddhist, Moslem, and female. It made for interesting days and nights in Suburban Boston. When Molly had to leave town on assignment, her sister Mary would take the girls. Mary was the wife of an American Airlines pilot, who was gone quite often and Mary loved the company in her pretentious, but childless home in Arlington. The arrangement worked on all levels as the girls loved their permissive Aunt Mary and the suspension of rules that their mom imposed.

Molly knew she needed to call Mary and set up yet another kid transfer, but she needed to talk to Harry Stompe immediately. She found his editor's door open as usual and him on the phone, waving her in. She didn't even try to listen to his end of the conversation, but rather, took a chair and looked out at the view of downtown Boston behind him. It was frigid on the East Coast and a kind of ice fog hovered over downtown, fed by thousands of emissions of heat and exhaust. She noticed that the sun, though slightly occulted by the gauzy layer was set like a gray pearl in the morning sky out over Logan. It had risen far south although she knew it was making its way back north. It was mid January and this new year would be special. She was awakened from her thoughts by the sound of the phone being hung up.

"I knew once Erin flew to you that you would fly to me. And I know what the sixty-four thousand dollar question is," chirped Harry.

"Why me?"

Harry nodded. "He asked specifically for you, Molly."

"I know that part now, but why me? We have no history, Harry. None. He doesn't know me from Adam...or Erin for that matter."

Harry looked at Molly, but neither spoke nor moved for a long moment. She stared back. Finally, he took a piece of paper from his desk and pushed it over to Molly. She looked, but did not reach for it.

"What's that?" It was a coy probe.

"It's your passport to adventure, Ms. Costello. Written in the hand of Roland Heinz, twice now winner of the Pulitzer Prize for Literature. It seems you have an admirer, Molly. Read this."

Molly picked up the single sheet of plain lined yellow paper and read it.

To Harry Stompe, editor-in-chief
Art Harvest Magazine
Boston

Hello Harry,
Long time no hear or see. Well, I suppose that is my fault. The hermit-writer image was not a planned thing, but rather evolved over time. You knew me

9

before I was even published so you know the other Roland Heinz. I miss both of us sometimes, though rarely. I received your request for an interview the other day and decided to grant it. Surprised? I'll bet you are. There have been similar requests from most of your mighty rivals, but then I got to thinking about the old days in Chicago and got sentimental. So, yes, you can send me one of your writers, but I get to pick which one. I found an article in one of your back issues written by a Molly Costello. The story was a review of an obscure novel by our old acquaintance C.M. Connell. Remember him? Anyway, some time ago Ms Costello wrote a scathing review of Connell's book, but seemed to, as an aside, capture the essence of my old friend. She read him like a book, so to speak. I find this to be a rare feat these days. The art of Capture. Send Ms. Costello my way if you want an interview, but make it soon. My mind can change like the weather in the Midwest. I look forward to hearing from you, Harry.
Sincerely;
Roland Heinz
Pipe, Wisconsin

Molly slipped the sheet back toward Harry. "Seems there is another story within the story, Harry."

Harry was always good at anticipating directional changes. "You mean what's my history with Heinz? I am sure you will ferret that out of him when you meet him."

Molly nodded off a smile. Her confidence was back. She was feeling a burst of excitement, but also trying to remember the article Heinz mentioned. She did not remember C.M. Connell on even a subliminal level. She decided it didn't matter.

"You'll need to leave today or tomorrow at the latest," he continued. "Is that a problem?"

"Not really. I already did a quick check on Heinz and located where he lives in Wisconsin, wherever the heck Pipe is. I had no idea. But, I booked a flight to Chicago for later today and then another hop to Milwaukee. I reserved a car there and googled a map to Pipe. I should make the flight with no problems."

"Except one, Molly. You will need to go back and double those reservations. I am sending Mike Gabler along with you as photographer."

The information threw Molly for a second. "Mike Gabler? Why are you using him, Harry? Not that I am disappointed, but my god, he's the best photog is New England. A staff photographer would do just as well, wouldn't it?"

"Actually, no. This is my decision. You obviously know Gabler's work. He is not a photographer, but an artist in camera medium. He's is the best. I want enough of your writing and his pictures to make a coffee table book on Roland Heinz down the road. Besides the interview for *Art Harvest*, I need enough material for that book."

"And you have Heinz's permission for all this?"

"Well, no, not really, but that does not go beyond this room. I am, you might say, looking ahead towards a foreseeable future."

Molly, nodded, thinking hard. "You mean something posthumous on Roland Heinz, don't you? Is there something I should know, Harry? Is this his first and last in-depth interview?"

Harry Stompe stood up and turned to his picture window. He folded his hands behind his back in a way that only men in their seventies can do. It is as though this posture alone exuded mature thought and contemplation. He then turned to face Molly. "He's a very old friend and I am not trying to exploit that fact. Two Pulitzer's is a rare feat, especially for someone who began his exceptional writing rather late in life. Heinz is very important not only to me, but to the world. He is a person who's past and inspiration is very much an untapped resource. His early efforts were ordinary to say the least and then wham! Two novels, both prize winners, Molly. What the hell does he have in reserve that will never be given to us in print? No matter what he's going to be a legend in American literature. I want to archive some of that. That's all."

"Harry, I wasn't questioning your motive. It's just that you might scare him off with Mike Gabler doing his camera magic and me, what, going beyond the depths of a simple interview? Do you really think someone so private all these years is going to open up like a...?

"Coffee table book?" inserted Harry. "No, maybe not, but I am asking you to be creative. This could be your Pulitzer, Molly Costello. And Mike Gabler's as well. I will leave it up to you. Think about it, okay? Think about your approach. This man will throw you out if he thinks you are not the person he thinks you are. And yes, he will probably not pose for Mike, but that's Mike's problem. When is your flight?"

"4:05 PM."

"Call me when you get to Milwaukee tonight. You will be staying there, I assume. Only a couple hours drive to where he lives, I believe."

"An hour or so."

"Good, go. My secretary will have your various vouchers before noon. Get her your flight details and she will make sure Gabler meets you at Logan. Any other questions?"

"Lots of them...all for Roland Heinz."

"That's my girl."

Molly Costello fought the giddiness of cloud nine the rest of the day as she made her arrangements. Something wonderful had blown in over the transom and she recognized how special it could be.

Molly's cell phone chirped while she was browsing the concourse bookstore at Logan. She had found one of Mike Gabler's photo essay books and was stunned to find herself holding it when his call came in. As she spoke to him she was looking at his picture on the back dust cover. She thought he was handsome, but a little artsy looking with the long hair and earring. She thought he looked like he could be nicknamed the Camera Pirate. She looked forward to meeting him.

Gabler would not be meeting her and the flight to Chicago, but he would catch up to her in Milwaukee about forty minutes after her flight arrived. They made arrangements to rendezvous and hung up. Almost immediately she got a call from her sister, putting the girls on to say good night and goodbye.

"Mom, where are you going again? asked Melanie.

"I'm off to Wisconsin, Mel. Do you know where that is?"

"It's in the middle and up." Melanie knew her maps, but was a little confused about directions.

"Well something like that. Listen, I want you and your sister to be good and listen to Aunt Mary. She's the boss, okay?"

Molly heard giggling and Melanie doing an aside to Mary. "You're the boss." Then Melanie dutifully handed off to Sonia. Her English was slightly stilted as African English often sounds. Molly found it endearing, like everything else her daughters did.

"When are you coming home, Mom?" asked Sonia.

"Soon, I hope, babe. But, hey, I haven't even left yet." Molly was going to expound on that idea some more when Sonia said a quick, 'okay, bye' and hung up. Just as well, the flight was being called. Molly quickly acknowledged an inner feeling of excitement. A feeling that this trip was going to be the one that made her bones. That thought alone lifted her into the air above Boson and turned her west into the early dusk of winter.

CHAPTER THREE

I never felt in control of my life. Not a day. Decisions based on intellect, experience, and intuition always turned to acrid smoke when I ignited them. I spent many an hour pondering luck and its cosmic origins, but nano-seconds on planning. It showed. I was born without brakes. I was a daredevil fascinated by a dervish of war. Spinning like a pinwheel galaxy fresh from the bang. But, then motion is never predictable or never-ending. As the emotional losses piled up so did the physical ones. Hard to maintain control when each step you take produces hot agony. My hips went first. Then my heart attacked me. The last was the cancer. Doc said they got it all the first time, but they didn't. There is some sort of poetry in being eaten alive by one's self. Those rogue cells belong to me and I have no control over them; except on certain days. Certain fine mornings.

Carrie Stirling sat up in bed and smelled the coffee. She never needed an alarm clock since her work day started so late, but she always set the programmed coffee maker to go off at 8AM just to get her going. She rolled out of bed already dressed for the chilly morning in flannel pajamas and wool socks. She would not be advertising for Victoria's Secret in that slumber wear, but then there was no one around to notice anyway. No one wanted her secrets last night. Her apartment above the butcher shop in Pipe looked down onto Highway 151 and she noticed that it had snowed a little more over night. The plows had been out early, but the drifts were noticeably higher and a fresher white. It was winter in Wisconsin and the toilet seat was a sharp reminder.

Being a bartender was certainly honest work for a thirty-eight year old woman with only a high school diploma, but it was the deadest of ends, too. Carrie was still pretty enough to earn extra tips from the taproom Casanova's, but she didn't like the way they looked at her. Men in snowmobile suits and hoodies were not necessarily connoisseurs of beauty, but she did manage to attract some appreciative stares. She had the local Nordic blue-eyed blonde looks, although there were some pewter streaks in her hair if you looked closely. She had all the tools in her athletic frame; had them since she was twelve, but so far she had only brought in louts and bumpkins and that included her ex, the long departed Crazy Ray Hitowski.

Crazy Ray, the charming guitar playing bastard caught a break and had hit the road to Los Angeles just after instigating the birth of Carrie's son, Raymond Jr. and yawning through a charade of a civil marriage ceremony. Somehow, beyond all of Carrie's predictions of failure, Ray had hit it big in the L.A. music scene. He had left a minimum wage factory job in Chilton and now he was making enough money to throw a lot of it away, but little to her as their kid grew up. They were only married on paper, but the child kept them in touch, sort of. It had all dragged on for years until Ray Jr. ran off to join his dad the summer before he would begin high school. Now Carrie was getting crazy, too. The insanity began with the coffee, the snow, the soaps, the drab meals, the bar, the leering drinkers, and ended in her bed. And then it started all over again. And then again. January was a calendar page that would be more useful starting a fire. It was damned cold in Carrie Stirling's world.

Last night had been a semi-typical night at the Back Room in Pipe, where she worked. Everyone called it the Bath Room, which seemed appropriate because the place stunk of piss, beer, and bleach. Oh, and cigarettes, too, but the whole state smelled like cigarettes so who noticed? Around ten thirty a group of eight or nine drunken snowmobilers rolled in and did a classic bar takeover. Bikers on sleds. Their women, of which there were three, were the drunkest and the loudest and one of them was using Carrie for an insult target. It began to get ugly and Carrie could not see any of her usual customers hanging around to lean on. It took courage to face down these harridans while their men drank and egged them on, but courage was something Carrie stored like firewood. One woman got so far into Carrie's face that her peppermint schnapps spittle was a four-letter aerosol of venom. When Carrie wiped the woman's face with a bar rag, the fight was on.

The first blow was blocked by Carrie as her assailant tipped it with a long windup. Drunks usually fight in slow motion, but Carrie noted this little bitch was pretty quick. But, not quick enough to evade the head butt that she delivered. Point blank. With a sound like a billiard ball being struck, the butt put the woman's lights out. Then with the speed of a gun-slinger Carrie pulled her cell phone and speed dialed 911. The Ski-doo merry makers almost fell over each other drag-ging the unconscious lady outside and making their getaway ahead of a potential breathalyzers of the County Sheriff. Curses and vows of revenge were lost in the roar of the fast getaway. All in a night's work and Carrie had the bruise on her forehead to prove it. If it didn't happen so often it might be slightly interesting to be in a bar fight, but it did and it wasn't. It was just Carrie Stirling's career.

Now it was 9AM on Saturday and her hands and feet were cold. Mr.Coffee promised to start her up. Oh God, help me, she whispered into her Packer's mug. Two hours later Carrie's mom, Pat dropped by after grocery shopping on Sat-urday and to have lunch. Carrie made a couple grilled cheese sandwiches and heated a can of tomato soup. They call this comfort food in Wisconsin, as if one could take comfort from starch, fat, and salt. More likely the comfort part came from the cold cans of Pabst Blue Ribbon.

"What happened to your head, Carrie?" Pat was going to ask about the bruise as soon as she walked in, but had waited for a volunteered explanation that wasn't coming.

"Little fight at the bar last night, Mom."

"He look worse than you?"

"It was a she and she looked like shit even before I nailed her. Let's change the subject, okay?"

That remark did change the subject, but it also brought silence to the table. The food and beer was making Carrie think about going back to bed. She had plenty of time before her shift started. She yawned at the top of the hour and her mom took the hint. She started to put her coat on and then turned back to her daughter.

"Hey, I almost forgot. I got something for you."

"What'd you get me, Mom?

Pat dug into her large purse and pulled out a well-used paperback book and handed it to Carrie.

"What's this?" Carrie was searching the cover for a clue.

"It's called *The Tap Root* by a man named Roland Heinz."

"Never heard of it or him. What's it about?"

"It's about...it's about time you read something besides that romance crap, that's what it's about."

Carrie gave her a tired smile and set the book down. She looked at the picture of the author on the back cover.

"This guy looks familiar."

"He should," said Pat with a wry smirk. "He only lives right up there behind you. The farm with the yellow barn on The Ledge."

"No shit! I've see that guy. He's a writer?"

"Not just a writer, dear. He just won his second Pulitzer Prize."

"A prize? So he's famous? Rich and famous?"

Pat opened the door and stood for a moment in the cold blast.

"He ain't too famous if no one around here ever heard of him but, I guess he must have some money livin' up there. But, you read that book, Carrie. It might just be something you can relate to. Better than drinking beer in the morning and watching them soaps."

"Like you don't?"

Pat slammed the door behind her and left Carrie stunned holding the mysterious book that was going to speak to her. She yawned and tasted the beer over the soup. It was a short walk back to the bedroom where she lay back down and located her glasses in the bedside table. She peeled back the cover and first few pages of the book and began to read the words of the neighbor that she sort of recognized. What she read amazed her and puzzled her so much that the nap never happened. She only noticed it was nearing time to go to work because darkness was beginning to creep into her room. It came with the cold again, but she realized there was a new source of warmth in her hands. The brief escape from the hammering noise of her reality left Carrie refreshed as only a good book could. It was the magic worked by the eye and the brain above a page, a straight shot of serenity.

CHAPTER FOUR

I knew I was starting to go either crazy or cosmic when I started taking the deaths of the road kills so hard. I would drive by a deer blown to pieces by a semi on the side of the highway and whisper to its ghost. I would tell it that things were going to be okay and that it could rest in my arms for a while if it needed to. I would imagine the animal sleeping in my lap, devoid of its final pain and no longer perplexed by its mystery. If this sounds foolish and sentimental, it is; but it is also, I decided, a form of compassion that was healing to me. It was like inventing a new religion while sitting in my truck, slipping down a highway of a world lost among the many others of the plan. If you look up at night and wonder what is going on up there, it seems logical that someone is looking down at us somewhere and wondering the same. My answer is I am here, mourning dead deer that were taken away, but now romp up there. Maybe some day we will all get to go home, no matter how many light years it is from the ditches of Highway 151.

Molly Costello was perched on a stool at one of the concourse bars at Mitchell Field in Milwaukee. She had noted that Mike Gabler's flight was delayed and had nothing better to do that to sip a Cosmo and do some more research on Roland Heinz. The bookstore at O'Hare had a very nice display rack of Heinz's latest, *A Winter Light* and she had bought a new hardbound copy. The book had been out for months, but the winning of the Prize had pushed it back out to the front of the stores. She knew from previous research that the book had not sold particularly well at first and her browsing was telling her why. The writing was too damned beautiful to be popular. Heinz had perfected the poetic novel and almost taken over the genre. As Molly sipped her magenta drink she noticed another reader next to her. This middle-aged business man was totally engrossed in an airport novel by a famous writer of pap. It made her ponder the mysteries of subjectivity and she knew most of the answers. What ever sold en masse was today's literature. Graphic novels were not anything new; they were the children of comic books. Spy and romance books were grown up Hardy Boys and Nancy Drew. Roland Heinz was from another planet. She never noticed the man who slid in next to her and sniffed her perfume, while reading over her shoulder.

"Ms. Costello, I presume," said a smiling Mike Gabler. Molly looked up with a start and saw one of the most pleasant faces she had ever seen. Very pleasant. Like the dust cover photo. Mike Gabler was shorter than she had imagined; more wiry. He had the same long shaggy hair as his photo, but the dust cover shot was black and white and this man was a blonde. He was wearing some fashionable glasses over his brown eyes in this, his real life visage.

"You're Mike. How did you know who I was?"

"Well, you said you would wait for me in the bar closest to my gate and who the fuck else is reading Roland Heinz around here?"

Molly looked at the book. '"Have you read this?"

"I skimmed the other prize winner. I found it in paperback for the flight. I can't say it grabbed me much, but then maybe it was because there weren't any pictures."

Molly looked surprised at first and then giggled. "Definitely no pictures in his books. But, you know there are some gorgeous images."

"I get the difference, Molly, but let's just say I am not much of a reader. I don't have time with my work."

"Busy?"

"Yeah, but I dropped everything when Harry called. I owe him one or two so here I am. By the way, where are we?"

Molly glanced around the airport bar, which doubled as a snack bar. Some people were wolfing sausages, while others were watching the sports report on the late news. "It's all about bratwurst and the Packers. We must be in Wisconsin."

"And beer," Gabler noted. "We got time for one or ten?"

Again Molly did her giggle. "Maybe one. We still need to find our rental car and then find the hotel. We're supposed to meet with Heinz around noon tomorrow."

"I didn't get any details except that I was supposed to hook up with you. You lead, I follow."

Molly was astounded by the number of metal cases that Mike had checked through baggage. She had not grasped before that the rental car that had been reserved for them was a mini-van, but was pleased with someone's foresight. The hotel was not far from the airport and the room reservations were held so the day was coming to an end on a quietly efficient note. As the porter wrestled with the cases, she began to bid good night to her photographer.

"Meet you for breakfast?" she asked.

"Sure," Gabler mumbled as he handed a generous tip to the porter.

"How about 8am in the lobby, Mike?"

"How about 9?" he said with a tired smile.

"Okay, that's fine. We don't have much of a drive tomorrow." Molly watched the baggage cart go into the door and thought of something else. "Don't you usually have one or two assistant cameramen?"

"I usually do, and a stylist...and a wardrobe person, but Harry thought too many people would spook Heinz."

"Can you manage all of this by yourself?"

"Actually, no, but I do have an assistant to help?"

"Who?"

"You."

Molly's smile froze and then melted into a moue. "I don't know the first thing about this gear, Mike. Besides, I will be busy doing my job. Are you going to double as my typist and editor?"

Mike, being the easy going guy he was, let out a chuckle as he searched the sky for a reply. It came. "Molly Costello, I'll do what ever I can to help you if you do the same for me. This is definitely going to be a different sort of gig for us. Let's try to have some fun and get it done quickly. Wisconsin in

January is not my idea of a winter vacation. Fast forward together, okay?"

Molly really liked him and was charmed by the breeziness, but didn't want to cede any ground on the first night. "How about forward slowly together? We can talk about how to get this job done in the morning. I'm too tired to think. Goodnight, Mike." She then turned and headed into the lobby in the direction of the elevator. Gabler followed, but veered off to the bar. He had bought himself an extra hour of sleep in the morning and intended to burn it tonight. He did, however watch Molly walk away and liked what he saw. A talent for gauging camera angles had developed into figuring out other complex angles in life, too. Molly had potential. Being single and in a new city made him eager to pursue other venues of potential in the lounge.

By early morning the sky had turned low and gray and a light snow was falling on southeast Wisconsin. As a life-long New Englander, Molly was not daunted by the promise of slick roads, but the grayness took some of the luster off of the assignment for some reason. As she looked out her hotel window and pondered this her cell phone chirped. It was Harry Stompe calling with some bad news. She took the call while sitting cross-legged sitting on the bed watching herself in the mirror. She was soon frowning.

Molly caught up with Mike in the coffee shop. He was already sipping coffee and seemed a bit red-eyed, which made him not quite resemble the affable goof he had been the night before. She sat down and accepted a coffee fill from a busboy. She was adding cream to it when she found her vocal approach to the day.

"I've got some bad news, Mike and you don't look like you're up to it," she began.

"What is that supposed to mean? The latter part."

"Well, I'm Irish and from South Boston so I know a hangover when I see one. That's your business, but..."

"Thank you," Mike interjected quickly. "What's the bad news? I assure you I can take it...in my condition."

Molly now smiled despite herself. Maybe the wounded Mike was okay, too. "Harry called and told me that Roland Heinz had to go to the hospital last night."

"No shit? Does this mean the whole thing is cancelled?" Mike sounded almost hopeful.

"Not necessarily. We are supposed to go up to his place as planned and see what happens. Harry was told that Heinz may be back home by this afternoon if all goes well. It seems he had to have a pacemaker adjustment or something like that."

"Oh."

"I kind of suspected from the way Harry talked to me before about this assignment that Heinz's health was an issue. There seemed to be some sort of unspoken urgency to all of this. Anyway, we are still go." Molly then lowered her head slightly to draw direct eye contact with Mike. "You hit the fun button a little hard last night?"

"Not sure I would say 'fun' per se. I met some locals in the bar who thought my accent was funny. And then having identified me as an outlander, turned me on to a couple of the local poisons. If self-poisoning is fun I had lots of it last night."

"What's the local poison?" Now Molly was grinning a smile way brighter than the day.

"Not too sure, but it seems the base of every drink around here is that Jaegermeister shit. Tastes the way bad Christmas cologne smells."

"You live and learn."

"May not live, but yes, I learned. Let's get going. I can't stand the smell of food right now."

Molly put down her menu and shrugged. They were on the freeway heading through Milwaukee a half hour later. The heatless sun had returned and the morning was bright and white.

CHAPTER FIVE

A long life can be suffocating. At my age I lie beneath an avalanche of moments, memories, and regrets of one kind or another. This bloating of experience is painful, especially when you see that the only way to let the air out of the bag is to die. It was always a precondition to everything we do, but millions of years of specie denial has created a formidable wall between where I have lived and where I will expire. Every time I tried to wrap my imagination around a heaven, I painted it with colors of happiness that were mixed in this world. This here one, Earth, where ever the hell we are. I have an address out on the mail box so that all the bill collectors and advertisers can locate me, but what is my real address? I wondered could God send me a letter? I decided it would be neighborly for me to send one or two to him first. An introduction. That letter became The Tap Root. My literature became better by great degrees when I knew who my reader was going to be. In truth, I wrote a letter to God because I never got one from anyone down here. That statement is not precisely true, but it is far from utterly false. I was lonely and went to the page with my head down, but I let it all go. Writing that book turned me inside out, which was just fine because my insides certainly required some airing.

It was Sunday and as usual Meg Bollander strolled down the steps of the Catholic Church in Johnsburg feeling spiritually uplifted and forgiven of her sins. The church steps were crunchy from the liberal application of rock salt and she held the handrail as not to slip on the ice-killing pellets. Last night's mere two inches of new snow gave the scenery a post card gloss that warmed her heart, even with the temperatures in the teens. Most of the parishioners departed in their cars to supper clubs and home, but a few headed across the street to the local bar to get a few under their belt before the Packer's playoff game, which was two hours away.

Meg, at sixty-five still had nothing against an eye-opener, but had always disdained the Sunday morning, post-mass drinkers. Today she took a few steps toward her car, but then had a second thought and headed across the street to Karl & Vi's Tap. The bar had been habituated from time to time by Roland Heinz and she was thinking someone might have some news about him. She had seen the ambulance at his place yesterday afternoon and was concerned, though she would neither admit it to herself or others. She wanted news, but had no prejudice as to whether it was good or bad. She sat down at the end of the bar next to an older woman who was clutching the rail with hands that looked like the talons of a perching bird. She wore a Packer head scarf covering curlers and Meg knew it was a mistake the second she turned towards her.

"I know you," the old woman croaked.

"Excuse me?" Meg mumbled. The bartender arrived at the same instant and she was flustered.

"What'll it be?" the bartender asked while staring at the overhead TV airing the endless pregame shows.

"Um, I'm not sure...maybe a Bloody Mary," Meg stammered, but quickly got herself on track. "Not too hot, with olives, please." The bartender nodded and moved away to make the drink. Meg then spoke to the woman beside her. "You know me from church?"

"I knew you from church, when I used to still go, and from a long time ago. You're one of the Bollander girls." Meg had not heard herself referred to in those terms in ages.

"Why yes, Meg Bollander. And you are...?"

"I'm old lady Dankermann, the village crone." The lady waited for a second for her introduction to sink in and then threw her head back and laughed. "You and your sister used to call me a witch!"

The light of recognition came on in Meg's mind. She remembered the woman and quickly calculated that she must be in her nineties. "Of course, I remember you. You lived in that old brick house on 151 in Pipe. We used to trick or treat there and you scared us. My god, that was over 50 years ago!"

"Something like that."

The bartender arrived with the Bloody Mary and Meg nodded to Mrs. Dankermann's Old Fashion indicating a refill was on her. "Well, I guess I don't need to ask how you are Mrs. Dankermann. You seem well."

The old lady paused, nodding until she got her fresh Old Fashion to her mouth and threw it down in two swallows, licked her lips and smiled. "One foot in this bar and the other in the grave, dear. But, I appreciate your sweet lie. How come a pretty young thing like you never got married?" She saw that her gear shift had confused Meg. "You got the same last name as when you were a girl."

Meg recovered. "Oh, well, yes and no. I was married for a few years." She saw the old lady raise an eyebrow. "When the sonofabitch left, I took back my name. Isn't Dankermann your maiden name?"

"Well, yes and no. You see I married my third cousin of the same last name. Folks did that sort of thing back then. It was hard to find a husband when you never got out of the county. Anyway, enough talk about crappy marriages. How do you like the Packer's chances today against them damned Lions?"

Meg tossed back her drink and pondered the question as the alcohol began to dance in her tummy. "They always beat the Lions, don't they?"

The old lady rubbed her withered chin. "I suppose."

The bartender was back as soon as his trained eyes spotted the empty glasses. This time he merely pointed at the glasses and raised his eyebrows. Meg shook her head, but the Mrs. Dankermann wanted another. Meg caught the bartender before he walked off.

"You know Roland Heinz, don't you?"

The bartender nodded and said, "Yep."

"I know he comes in here and I was wondering if anyone knew what happened to him last night?' Meg asked.

"Haven't seen Rollie in a while," said the bartender. "Something happened to him?"

There was an ambulance out at his place last night. I was just wondering if anyone knew about it."

The bartender shrugged, shook his head, and went to get the old lady her drink.

"If the ambulance come for him then he must be in the hospital," said Mrs. Dankermann. "Why don't you call the hospital if you want some news, dear?"

The woman's logic was not lost on Meg, but she had hoped to get some local intelligence without making that call. It seemed like a good time to leave before any strange conversations developed. "I guess I should. Listen, Mrs. Dankermann, it was nice running into you. Enjoy the game. I had better get home now."

Mrs. Dankermann was already at her fresh drink and nodded, while signaling a 'ta ta' with her free hand. Meg fled from the bar and quickly noticed how fresh the air was on the outside. Every iota of good sense she had told her to leave Roland Heinz to his fate and put him out of her mind. She had done it many times before. But, then she had just finished reading *A Winter Light* the night before last and could not get him or the book out of her mind. How could the man she loathed with all her broken heart have written such books?

Meg drove back to her farm, all the while cursing the wind turbines that ruined the view of her parcel of the Holyland. The Wisconsin Holyland was the strip between Lake Winnebago and Lake Michigan in which most of the tiny towns were named after saints. The tall white modern wind machines seemed to be a heretical blight on such a spiritual landscape. Intellectually she understood the need for clean energy and how these monstrosities were harbingers of the future world; but why did they have to show up here? With most of her life in ruins brought down by the past, how could this last mark be put on the present. These thoughts made her angry every time she went outside and saw the windmills and heard their throb. Even at night she felt her blood pressure rise as she saw the synchronized blinking of their red lights competing with the stars. And then there was that last one they erected; the one closest to her property. It was all the more horrendous for her that it was on Roland Heinz's land. Roland, the horrible man and beautiful writer. Damn him, she thought. Gatsby had his green light at the end of Daisy's dock and she had her winking red light, two hundred feet up and forty feet inside his property line. Her Bloody Mary had already turned to bile in her stomach.

When she got home she made a discreet call to St. Agnes Hospital in Fond du Lac and learned that Roland Heinz had been released that afternoon. She hung up and thought, well at least he didn't die. At least he didn't die before she could curse him again for how he had ruined her life and how he was continuing to trouble her. It was only mid-afternoon, but already the sun was getting low over the southwest corner of Winnebago. Thank God, the wind turbines were not down to the lakeshore, she thought. The view of the sun beginning to lay a silver trail on the snow and ice was a spiritually blown kiss to the senses. Meg sat in her rocker facing the window and pulled an afghan over herself. She told herself she would just rest her eyes, but when she opened them again it was as dark as a tomb outside and inside her house. She got up and went to the kitchen see about making some supper. She snapped on the small TV on the counter and saw that the Packers had just lost to the Lions. More disappointing men from Wisconsin.

CHAPTER SIX

I arrived in Southeast Asia in 1964 unprepared. I suppose my self-inflicted post war wounds have diluted most of the carnage I witnessed, but not quite enough to keep some of it out of my dreams. Every once in a while I stroll that wet, green dream scape and come across the bloated bodies of those four Vietnamese children. I turned away pretty fast, but saw enough to know that they were traveling together and one of them stepped on a mine. I never assigned blame to whatever side planted that explosive where kids could wander over it because it didn't matter. It made me ashamed to be a human being, a member of the species that could create that scene. Karin said I had changed after I got back to Wisconsin and I had, but I couldn't really define how. She could. I was never much of a drinker and then I became an expert. I disdained the hippies and their drugs and then became one. I shined up my combat medals with alcoholic spit and shoved them down the throats of my friends. It took me many years to figure out which side I was on in that war and by the time I did, it was too late. They might have just as well put my name on that black wall in DC, but instead they put my name on some divorce papers that marked the death of everything that used to be me. Poor Karin. And the war didn't kill my love, I did. The person inside me, then and now, is me.

Roland Heinz sat in the lobby of St. Agnes Hospital and waited for his ride home to arrive. He was feeling pretty good considering how bad he had felt on Saturday evening. He had felt the rhythm of his heart change and had driven down to the end of his drive, thinking he could make the trip to ER on his own. When he began to sweat in the near zero temperatures, he dialed 911 on his cell phone and waited for the ambulance. This condition had occurred before and he reminded himself that he shouldn't be driving and possibly endangering someone else. There was about a twenty minute wait for the paramedics, every second of which was spent in mortal contemplation. Once inside the warm ambulance he was able to joke with the EMT's and come back down to earth. He remembered that the woman from the magazine was coming out the next day so he had called Harry Stompe on the way in. He told Harry to tell his people to come up as planned as he didn't think the pacemaker adjustment would keep him more than over night.

The following morning, he got the idea that Ms. Costello could begin her assignment by picking him up at the hospital and taking him home. He thought it would be a good way for them to get to know each other under somewhat strange circumstances. He even smiled when he thought that it would give her a great angle for starting her story. *I met Roland Heinz at the hospital the day after his heart's mainspring had gotten rewound.* Something like that. He learned from Harry that there was a photographer coming along, too, which threw him a bit. He didn't like that idea, but Harry's assurances finally made sense to him. When he heard it was Gabler, he was pretty sure he was going to die. Why else would the best photographer in the US be coming along if not for a parting shot. When a mini-van pulled up to the entrance and a lovely and concerned woman got out of the passenger side, he knew she had to be Molly Costello. He watched her activate the automatic doors and enter with a gust of frozen air and something about her melted his ailing heart. She searched the lobby and immediately locked onto him. They both smiled and Roland gave a timid wave. In a moment so rare that the odds of it happening can only be calculated in astronomical terms, two strangers from different ages and lives became instant friends. Roland stood up to greet her and they both knew a handshake would be too formal. They hugged like a long lost father and daughter.

Mike had gotten into the back seat allowing Roland to ride shotgun. The introductions had been brief, but now on the way to Ghost Farm, the atmosphere was warming. Roland smiled at Molly and leaned over the seat to Mike.

"Sorry if I put a cramp in your plans. I know this is quite irregular," Roland stated sheepishly.

"No, no, Mr. Heinz. I often meet my subjects at the hospital," Mike quipped.

"Better than the morgue," Roland said.

Mike noticed there was a light in his eyes that projected health and life. It seemed strange to observe such a thing in under these circumstances. He wanted to photograph him right that second as he looked with the late afternoon sunlight on his face. Mike hated to miss such a moment, but it was gone already. Roland had turned to Molly. He gave her some quick driving directions. It was almost dark, but the sky had a lingering winter twilight that allowed the new snow to glow with a fey light.

"In about another mile you can start looking for a pair of blue reflectors on the right. That'll be my driveway. Did Harry tell you that you are staying with me?"

Molly looked in the rearview mirror at Mike. "No, he didn't. As a matter of fact, we have hotel reservations in Fond du Lac at the Executive Suites, right Mike?" As much as she and Roland had connected she was not prepared to be his house guest. It was not as absurd as it was a surprise that caught her off guard. Mike didn't say a word.

"You can call and cancel when we get home. There, turn right here," said Roland. They passed the mailbox marked with a fire number and the stenciled words, 'Ghost Farm' and headed up hill to the farm house. The tires came to a crunching halt on the crystalline snow and both

Molly and Mike craned to look at the house as Roland got out fumbling with his keys. Slowly the other two got out, their gazes fixed on the scene. In the last light of day, it looked too charming for words. Molly felt a sense of coming home. Mike wanted to take a picture, and he quickly did with small digital camera. He took several in rapid succession.

Molly and Mike followed Heinz in through the porch and into the living room. Molly's grin became painted on her face as she took the place in. It was simply the most cozy, charming room she had ever seen. There was also a strong sense of déjà vu, that she would explore later. Roland went through the house turning on lights that did not so much light the rooms as decorate them. In the kitchen he dropped his keys on the table and turned to his guests.

"I had a cleaning lady come in a couple days ago. It doesn't always look this nice, but it does look nice doesn't it?" Mike and Molly nodded. "Okay, who wants a drink besides me?"

Mike's hand popped up reflexively, but Molly's motherly side came out. "Are you sure you should, you know, have a drink Roland? We just picked you up from the hospital."

"All the more reason, girl." He paused and collected his thoughts. "Listen, thanks for your concern, but I have my own rules. Molly, Mike, if you got a peek at my medical records you would understand that preventative health measures don't apply to me anymore. Okay? There is not an organ in my body that is not under attack and the only time my afflictions take a time out is when I have a nice civilized drink. Doing it in my kitchen makes it all the more civilized. So, again, who wants a drink."

"What do you have? asked Molly, now smiling.

"You name it."

"Wine?"

"Of course. Red or white?"

"The latter," answered Molly.

"And you, Mike?"

"I'll have whatever you're having, Mr. Heinz."

"Good. Red wine for the lady and frozen Jaegermeister for the men." He went into a walk in pantry and Molly could scarcely control her laughter. She gave Mike a good natured elbow and leaned into him in a gesture that was something between a hug and a push. A minute later they were seated around the kitchen table. Molly had just hung up her cell phone having cancelled the hotel rooms in town. She glanced at her watch and realized it was too late to call the girls back east. It bothered her a little, but she put it out of her mind. She was beginning to form a vague outline for the Roland Heinz interview and story. It was unfolding before her eyes.

"You couldn't reach your daughters, Molly?"

"I didn't try. Too late back there."

Roland thought for a moment. "We should bring them out here. My treat. This project will take a little time, right? I think you should have your girls here with you."

Molly didn't know how to reply. Surely Roland was talking through his drink. And yet, there was a hint of insistence in his tone. What exactly was this man saying to her? She decided not to reject the idea out of hand, but wait and see if it was still on the table in the morning. The offer did, however, make her miss the girls all the more.

"Let me think about it over night, Roland," she offered. "I am going to have a lot of work to do in a short time here."

"Well, my dear, I told Harry that this was not going to be a hit and run interview. I expected you...at least you, Molly, to be here for at least a week or ten days."

Molly was stunned, but again did not want to end the day with a conflict of ideas.

"Well, I work for Harry so what ever he says...and you, too, of course."

The evening ended in small talk and yawns.

After Roland had shown Molly and Mike where they would sleep and the basics for navigating the house, he succumbed to his own fatigue and went to his studio in the cheese shed, where he spent most of his nights. There was a wood-burning stove in the building and he soon had it stoked and beginning to warm enough space near a couch so he could sleep comfortably. The temperature outside had slipped down into single digits and with the cold came a profound silence, as though all the entire world was frozen solid.

Molly, too, was exhausted and found the suggestion of bed to be seductive. Her room upstairs had a high, ancient bed covered with a yellowing white chenille bedspread and when she sat down on it, it made a rusty groan. She could almost imagine a pile of corroded bed spring metal flaking onto the floor below her. With little exploration and minimal undressing, Molly fell into bed in this strange place vowing to see what it was all about in the morning. Only Mike remained up past ten o'clock and he was restless.

Looking out of his bedroom window at the front of the house, he looked down the drive to Highway 151. There was almost no traffic this time of night, but he did see some colored neon down about a half a mile to the north. It was a beer sign and that meant a bar. He talked himself into the premise that a walk in the cold would set him up for a good night's sleep. He knew he was lying to himself, but he did it often enough to not be conflicted. He wanted some company and a nightcap and was willing to brave foreign and frozen ground to get them.

CHAPTER SIX

One common kindness affixed to life in the upper Midwest is that we enjoy all four of the seasons. Sometimes this compliment is backhanded by the observation that winter dominates about half of that year. It's a local joke, which I believe was primarily designed to keep people from other parts of the country from falling love with our well kept secret. The changing seasons play so much to the emotions that the taciturn northerner is hard pressed to express how the soul dances in step with the trees and wild flowers, the birds and animals of the land. There is always one day in each season that subliminally brings back the very same day in a lost childhood. Whether smelling grass after a thunderstorm, shuffling feet through fallen leaves, or watching snow pile up around a warm house; it strikes the most profound chord. I find my sublime moment in the woods of a winter day when the sun is just about to bow out to the stars. There is a pastel rainbow of hues in the sky and upon the snow that touches me so sweetly. I seek out those moments now rather than stumble across them, much like someone in pain seeks a remedy. In the quiet, stark amethyst woods I find myself as I was a boy; innocent again and full of wonder.

"Oh no!" Carrie shrieked. She had just gotten out of the shower and was beginning her pre-work ritual for Sunday night when she caught sight of herself in the mirror. Somehow during the night after her Saturday shift, the course of the bruise had taken a turn and evolved into the dreaded raccoon effect. There were now dark blood circles around her eyes and no makeup trick was going to fix it.

It really didn't matter, she knew. There was no one to sub for her at such short notice, especially for such a lame excuse. She knew that she would be the butt of every joke tonight, but the jokesters were all known to her and harmless. In order to counteract her ridiculous face, she decided to dress up the rest of her; maybe draw a little attention to below her neck. She chose a low cut white sweater that was just flimsy enough to allow a black bra to be seen through it. Perfect, she thought as she added a little perfume for further effect. Again she went to the mirror.

"Oh great," she said aloud to her image. "A sexy raccoon. My god!"

Carrie made sure the apartment was shut down for the night and also ready for her to flop back into it after her shift. It was part of the ritual. Nothing ever changed. Just before she turned off the bedroom light she saw the book on the bed stand. She had spent the last two days absorbed in it, when she was not at work. She had a pleasant, fleeting thought that maybe there was something to come back to later. It was a thought both foreign and yet interesting. How could a book make you want to come home, get into bed, and spend some time allowing it to make pictures in your mind? It was a subtle change in the routine and she liked it.

Mike Gabler realized about a hundred yards from the Ghost Farm driveway that he was grossly underdressed for this kind of weather. He had a light wool shirt under a thin down vest and the frozen air was leaking into his skin everywhere. At least, he noted, it was a calm night. Wind chill factors might be lethal. He tried to keep his blurry eyes focused on a white and green Heineken sign hanging above the door of a brick building. Please don't close before I get in there, he though as he crossed the last quarter mile. He saw a couple cars and trucks parked out front and as he got to the front of the building he saw the warm lights inside the pub and the figures of a few people seated at the bar.

Despite the cold he stood outside and studied the scene for a moment. To his camera eye is looked so wonderful, so Americana. He loved every pub and bar he had ever been in and always looked forward to the next. He liked his drinks, but it was something more. To an only child, an orphan, a single man without children the bars felt like home. It was hard to explain, even to himself. He also knew that he often fell in love with bartenders, the female ones. As he walked in out of the cold every eye turned to him, just as he would have scripted it.

Mike nodded and said hello and then looked at the bartender. He saw the sweater first because that's where his roving eye landed first, but then he found her face. Like a flashing sign in his brain he plainly saw the message that his eyes were sending to his heart. "I love you Owl-eyes." Mike Gabler, the best photographer in New England had found his Mona Lisa in a rustic bar in Pipe, Wisconsin. He took a seat at the empty end of the bar near the door, where no one wanted to sit because of the draft and settled in. He fingered the small digital camera resting in his vest pocket.

Carrie Stirling was embarrassed when the new guy walked in. She was prepared for the ribbing she was getting from the regulars, but had not counted on some nice looking stranger, who was obviously staring at her bizarre mask of bruises. She threw a bar rag over her shoulder and ambled down to his seat at the bar, deciding that the tough girl approach would work better than the coy one.

"Hi, what can I get you?" she inquired. "And don't stare at my face. I know what I look like tonight." She couldn't help but smile at her own candor. His gorgeous smile was all over her.

"I'll have a Bacardi and Coke please. And you look just fine to me."

"Ba-Kah-di? What is that, a New York accent?"

"Actually, it is Baah-ston, but you're close."

Carrie made a cute pivot and went to make Mike's drink. The raccoon eyes did put her at a disadvantage, but she was letting him take a long look at the rest of her package. The bar flirt in her had shown up unexpectedly and her mind was racing with her hormones all of a sudden. The guy had passed the wedding ring check, there was none, and he had laid a fifty on the bar. Most of her patrons brought their pocket change out for their beers. A tip was unheard of. Mr. Baahston had definite possibilities. She glanced at the clock. It was 11:05. She had hoped that the local drinkers would head home early so she could close, but now she was calculating how much time she would have to work on this guy before the legal closing time.

There was a predator that lurked in Carrie at times like these. Pretty pink thoughts of love were nowhere to be found. It was the lust of a female panther cutting a delicious looking piece of meat from a herd. It was a well-honed ritual that she had perfected. When Carrie Stirling wanted to take a guy home she usually bagged him. When she brought the guy his drink she dipped down and gave him a preview of coming attractions. His eyes stepped into the snare willingly. Carrie was a beautiful crude diamond in a very deep rough.

As the few local rustics drifted home, Carrie and Mike found themselves alone. It was now around one AM and Mike caught Carrie looking at the clock.

"You don't have to stay open for me, Carrie," he said. The introductions and name exchanges had taken place long ago. They had pretty much run the gamut of banalities as the regulars had observed. They had seen Carrie's moves before and envied the new guy, but in this case her reputation was a source of pride. The old farmers knew there was nothing like a good red-blooded Wisconsin girl. They all had older versions waiting for them at home.

"Well, I can close early if there are no customers, so you would have to leave for me to close up."

Mike smiled and walked directly to the door and went out into the cold. He then appeared in the window, rapped on it and waved to Carrie. She already loved this guy, so she reached behind the cash register and flashed the house lights. Mike came back in a second later.

"Last call, Mike."

"Is there anything I can do to help you close?"

"Just sit there and wait. I have this down to a science.

Five minutes later Carrie was locking the front door and they faced a moment of reckoning on a quiet and cold sidewalk. Carrie pointed across the street to the meat market and the apartment above it.

"I live up there."

Mike loved the irony that she lived above a meat market.

He instantly realized his role in the metaphor and mooed. She laughed and pushed him into the street. Love in twenty-first century Wisconsin was pretty uncomplicated on a freezing January night at bar time. People who had been total strangers a couple hours before were going to get the intimacy of attraction out of the way before anything like common sense could ruin the night. She took his hand and walked him over and up to her bed. The stars were amazingly bright.

Mike woke up and checked his watch. It was almost 5 AM and he was a little disoriented. He could not quite remember where the bathroom was and it was pitch black in Carrie's room with the drapes closed. He sat up and allowed his eyes a few moments to adjust. There was a crack of dim light coming from under a door across the hall. He now remembered a Donald Duck night light plugged into the socket by the bathroom sink. He found the duck and the toilet now with little difficulty. When he came back into the bedroom, Carrie was snoring softly and he decided not to crawl back into bed. He remembered he was on Eastern time internally and knew he would never get back to sleep. He found his clothes in a lump by the bed and got dressed in the bathroom. After the love making session he had enjoyed a couple hours ago he wanted to at least leave Carrie a note. He tore off a page from a magazine and found a pen in his jacket pocket. He wrote a brief thank you note in the bathroom with a promise to stop by the bar later that night. He wanted to leave it somewhere where she would find it when she woke up so he let a shaft of light out of the bathroom so he could navigate the bedroom.

Mike found a book next to her pillow on the bed table and slipped the note just inside, leaving most of it hanging out. In the semi-darkness he noticed that it was one of Heinz's novels. Perfect, he thought. Symmetry, poetry, hot sex. He almost stooped to kiss her, but at this stage his escape was more urgent than a little sugar. He stepped away quietly, shut off the light in the bathroom, found the stairway down the back of the building, and headed back down Highway 151 to Ghost Farm. A couple dogs barked in the predawn, but they were the only sound on the road except for Mike's footsteps. It had been quite a night in Pipe. Good name, he thought with a smile.

When he got back up to the farm house there was the first glimmer of dawn to the east behind the barn. Mike was about to sneak back in the back door when he heard a soft whistle. He looked back toward the shed and saw Roland standing in the door, waving him over. Instinctively, before he walked over, he pulled out his small camera and took a quick picture of the old man, backlit by the light coming from within the shed and the shed backlit by the rosy promise of morning. It would later be recognized as the back cover photo of the coffee table book that Harry Stompe had conceived. Mike Gabler had earned his pay for the day in the instant before it began.

CHAPTER SEVEN

I watched paralyzed as my careful collection of friends began to leave me. It was like standing on a train platform as car after car of familiar faces pulled away and headed down a track I could not follow. Death and the simple circumstances of life were their tickets to that train and I could never understand why I was left behind, with the exception of Karin. I sent her off on another train in another direction. Solitude was an enemy before it became a friend. If you want to know who you truly are then live alone for several years. Live in a bottle. Live in a vacuum. Live in the dust and dirt of your own making. Live in the regrets. Live in the drawer of old photographs. Live in the cracked dishes and stained mugs. Live in sour sheets and musty blankets. Watch your skin yellow with the drapes. Live with the white noise of the universe collapsing back in upon itself. Then one day you see a way out. An opening so impossibly small that you will have to make yourself infinitely small to pass through it. You know you need to pass through the eye of the needle and you know it is going to hurt like hell. You have a choice of death's abyss or life's agony. Your only guidance is the sad, beckoning sound of a far off train.

"Com'on in, Mike. I got the coffee on and you look like you could use a cup." Roland had spotted Mike walking up the drive early Monday when he had gone outside his writing studio to take a leak in the snow. The only indoor bathroom on the farm was upstairs in the main house and it was too much trouble to take at that time of day just for a simple pee.

"Good morning, Mr. Heinz. Coffee sounds perfect," said Mike. He went into the shed as Roland held the door. Once inside, he again felt that urge to photograph what he saw. The room exuded warmth and the smell of strong coffee enhanced the anticipation of daybreak.

"You have to call me Roland, Mike. If you are going to be snapping my picture all the time we might as well be on familiar terms."

Mike looked at the camera still in his hand. "Do you mind this, Roland?"

"A little." Roland poured a cup of coffee and handed it to Mike. "I see a picture being taken and my mind immediately projects it into the future. You could show me that image right now and it would mean little. Years from now it might mean a lot. Maybe too much"

"I think I know what you mean. Some people are in love with the idea of being captured and others merely feel like captives. That's mainly why I specialize in landscapes and inanimate curiosities."

"I've seen your work and don't bullshit me. You do it all well and Harry didn't send you here to photograph just the sunsets. He likes the way you shoot people and turn them into curiosities. People buy what they cannot make themselves, right?"

Mike sipped his steaming mug. "Okay, no bullshit. I had that talk with Harry. He wanted me because he thought I photograph the way you write. His words. It sounded a little sketchy to me, but maybe he's smarter than I am?"

"He's sly. The foxes around here are stupid compared to Harry. He is in the process of marketing me and all of us here are just part of his plan. He's always been way ahead of the curve in his business. That alone doesn't get you and Molly into my house, but he is an old friend. A rare old friend. That's your ticket, Mike."

Mike nodded and walked to the windows facing east. "I will have to use some more intrusive camera equipment in here and around the farm. Will you be able to deal with that without being intimidated? If I have to use only this small hand-held, I won't be getting my job done."

"I will try to trust you and try to make you invisible. Just don't ask me to pose."

"Got it," Mike said, though he knew he would have to eventually.

"And never ask me to say 'cheese!'" Saying this, the true Roland Heinz emerged and spilled out from his slow-smiling eyes. Mike saw it and wanted to grab it, but let this one pass.

The Ledge

The sun was leaking into the room from The Ledge behind the farm and a moment occurred that was just too magical to photograph. Roland winked and went to a drawer and pulled out a pint of whiskey and poured a tad into each coffee mug. Both men turned toward the sunrise and swallowed a muddy toast to their new friendship. Roland wanted some details of Mike's exploits the night before and they pulled up chairs and propped up feet for the tale.

Molly was up and on the phone early to Harry Stompe. She explained Roland's strange suggestion about the girls coming out to get Harry's take.

"Molly, I think we should do whatever he wants."

"But, Harry, the girls are in school. My sister would have to get them packed. All that stuff."

"You let me take care of it all on this end. I will talk to Roland this morning and see what he is thinking. There is usually a careful reason behind everything he does. I will get Monica to make the arrangements for the girls. If they are indeed going to meet up with you, she will fly with them and drive them up there. They might be with you by supper time. You know Monica, the original mother hen."

Monica Beard had been Harry's personal secretary for thirty years. She was a jewel. Molly had no qualms about the girls being under her care. "Okay, call me back as soon as you speak to Roland."

"I promise. Hey, how is he? How is the farm?"

"Well, he is holding up remarkably well considering we picked him up from the hospital. He was the perfect host last night. As for this place...it is like a dream, but then you know that, don't you? I saw a picture of you on the refrigerator door taken in this house."

I was there a few years ago. It is awesome. The girls would love it."

"We'll see."

"Is Roland there right now?"

"I think I am alone. Roland slept in his studio and Mike went out and didn't come back last night. I think he is some-thing of a party boy in his spare time."

"I've heard that, but he's my choice on this deal. Problems?"

"Oh no, none. I really like him. Talk to you later, okay?"

"Yes, bye for now."

Molly did a little snooping in the kitchen looking for coffee fixings. There was a faint smell of cinnamon toast. She was suddenly hungry, but decided to go for a short walk before she did anything else. A morning walk was habitual for her and helped her set her head for the day. She dressed as warm as she could and headed out. The morning was amazingly clear, with just a sliver of a moon hanging low in the southwest. She took in a couple of lungfuls of frigid air and walked toward the yellow barn. She thought she smelled coffee coming from somewhere. She decide to leave the barn exploration for sometime when Roland could guide her and found a path leading down a tree line heading east onto the flats above The Ledge.

The terrain of this part of Wisconsin was vastly different from New England; certainly the parts of suburban Boston where she walked. The snow was not deep so ground features were discernable. Most of the large stones had been moved by some early farmer to the edges of the fields forming partial walls. Where there were gaps there was the ever-present barbed wire. No livestock was visible here, but she and Mike had seen thousands of black and white dairy cows coming up from Milwaukee. Molly noticed there was a farm house and barn behind and above Roland's place and it seemed to be a non-working farm, too.

As she walked along the stone wall toward a grove of trees, she was surprised and pleased to see three deer standing at the edge of the woods staring at her. She stopped for a moment as they watched each other. The mood was quickly broken by the noise of an engine. As the deer evaporated into the trees, Molly saw a red ATV coming toward her. As the small vehicle got nearer, she could see it was a woman. She waited to see if she had somehow wandered into a place she was not supposed to be, but then saw the woman driver was smiling as he pulled up. The engine was cut and the woman quickly got off and walked up to Molly.

"Good morning. I didn't expect to find a young woman in my field this morning."

Molly gave an embarrassed smile. "I am so sorry. I was just out for a walk."

"No need to apologize. My name is Meg Bollander. I live back there." Meg turned and pointed to her house and then her eyes shifted to over Molly's shoulder. "You come from down there?"

Molly turned around and saw the yellow barn. "Yes, I am staying down there."

"You're Roland Heinz's house guest?"

Molly was about to say something like, 'do you know Roland?' but then quickly figured everyone must know everyone around here. "Uh, yes, I am staying there, but it has to do with business mostly. I just met him yesterday, actually."

"And you are...?"

"Oh gosh, I'm sorry...again." Molly exhaled a nervous laugh. "I'm Molly Costello. I'm a writer for *Art Harvest* magazine." She instinctively pulled off her right mitten and extended it to Meg. Meg smiled and pulled off her glove to respond.

"Molly and Meg. We are both closet Margaret's, I take it," said Meg.

"Interesting way to put it, but yeah."

"Molly, would you like to hop on and come have coffee with me? I have known Roland longer than any living person in this county." The statement was true, but had a slight shade of dark irony and Molly as heard it and was interested.

"Might be interesting, Meg, but I don't have much time."

"That's okay, none of us do."

Meg showed Molly how to hang on to her and they drove off slowly across the bumpy ground towards Meg's house. Molly had a brief flicker of a thought that she was being taken away by the enemy, but set it aside. Conflict meant story angles and she needed a few. Her walk might turn out to be lucky.

CHAPTER EIGHT

Writing has always seemed like a kind of code that starts tapping out when you wander through the labyrinth of the imagination. I know I see something deep inside me and then I must find the words to describe it. I cannot begin to tell you how much good decoding I have done that has never made it to the page. Something beautiful can be whispered in your ear from a deep voice you've never heard before. You are caught without your writing tools and you tell yourself you will remember it all later. But, most often that instant passes never to come again. Just as often, surrounded by all your tools, the voice is silent. This is when the good writer begins his work. Now not only must the voice be invented, but the code must be constructed in a way that no other writer has ever conceived of it. Slowly the brain begins to fire and reaches down into the fingers. Sometimes just one added word to an ordinary sentence does the trick. When it happens I see the aura on the page and wonder where it came from. The old Celtic priests called Him, The Swift Sure Hand. He was the writer who wrote all that we have copied later under our own names.

When Carrie awoke and found Mike's note she was furious, mostly at herself. How could she sleep through his exit? The seduction had been easy, successful, and exciting, but now it seemed it had ended before it could develop beyond the one night. She got up and looked for any other signs of his presence. She always left something behind on purpose when she spent the night at some guys place to insure they would at least talk again. Mike had left her place like a professional thief leaves a crime scene, clean. Even the toilet was clean, she noted, which put him in a class way beyond most of her partners. She returned to bed and read the note again searching for hidden meanings, there were none. But, then she remembered something he had mentioned last night. He was a photographer in town working with a writer from a magazine. What on God's white earth would a magazine be covering in Pipe? The connection came slowly to her foggy brain as she began to suspect she was holding the clue in her hand. Of course they were here for Roland Heinz. It sure as heck wasn't for the local polka band. Hadn't her mom mentioned that he had won some sort of prize? She concluded that Mike was not so lost after all and was probably catching up on his sleep behind her on The Ledge. The house with the yellow barn. She drew her curtains on the east side of her apartment and was almost painfully blinded by the light. She squinted, but could not quite see the Ghost Farm from her angle, but she was certain he was up there. He said in the note he would see her again and she could now be pretty certain that he would. There was nothing else to do in Pipe. Carrie snuggled back into her bed and picked up the book. She had been fascinated by Heinz's writing before, now she was mesmerized. The book had suddenly become holy to her.

There was no sense of an enemy camp when Molly walked into Meg's kitchen for their exploratory conversation. The room, the whole house was filled with Wisconsiniana. And it was all so tidy. Each ceramic Holstein, gingham goose, Packer bobble head, and Badger curio somehow blended together into a charming mélange of collected memories and treasures. Meg saw Molly taking it all in and handed her a mug of coffee as her prowling had led her into the living room.

"Yeah, I know the knickknacks are maybe a little too much, but what can I do? I treasure them all in some small way," Meg said almost apologetically.

"No, I mean, this is all so neat. I can only imagine the time and care that went into all of this." Meg accepted the cup, noting it had Brett Favre's image on it. "Thanks."

"You know, I have been to a lot of places around here," Meg continued, "farm houses mostly, and you see a lot of this stuff. I think it has more to do with pride than any sense of kitschy art. We Cheeseheads think this is the center of the universe because most of us haven't gotten so much as a glimpse of the rest of the cosmos. Or even Chicago." Meg giggled stiffly at her own wit. She wasn't quite sure that Molly got her premise. Molly mumbled something and nodded, which convinced Meg that she had gone over her head.

As the ladies went back into the kitchen and found their places at the kitchen table, Molly switched her professional writer switch into the on position. "What kind of a neighbor is Roland Heinz?"

Meg stared at Molly for a very long moment. She quietly, but resolutely set her mug down and composed her thoughts. Molly waited with studied patience. She knew a nerve had been struck by lightning and she waited for the thunder.

"I was going to say, I don't know where to begin," Meg stated, "but, actually I do." She got up and walked over to the window and pointed her finger at some distant place. "Roland fucked me in that cornfield back in May of 1963." She turned back to Molly to record the shock effect. She saw it.

"I'm not sure which field or car he fucked my sister in the first time, but it was probably within a mile of my lost virginity." More shock.

"Now I realize, dear, that this was long ago and qualifies as ancient history, but you are not going to get that kind of insight down there at that ridiculous Ghost Farm."

Molly nodded thoughtfully, but she was mostly wishing she had her tape recorder. This was great stuff, even if she might not be able to use it. "Sounds like you have issues with our Pulitzer Prize winner."

"I don't have any issues with Roland the writer. Never did. But, the writer is also the man that condemned me to a life of collecting deer antler cutlery and miniature cardinals. He helped me collect a revenge husband who was a worse man than him. He led me to collect a latent taste for Kessler's Smooth as Silk Whiskey and he put an edge on me like a hunting knife."

Molly could see the anger sparking in Meg's eyes. Meg's hands were now on her hips in the classic stance of a scold.

"Maybe I should go...?" Molly said. It was a maybe a question, maybe a segue to the door.

Meg caught herself and seemed to soften and melt back into her kitchen chair. Her eyes twitched as the irises relaxed. "Oh god, I am so sorry. Oh, Molly, what you must think of me."

"It's okay. I have had some men in my life that cause the same reaction. But, I will say your fuse is short, Meg."

Meg mood was changing too rapidly. There were now tears in her eyes. "I love his writing. Particularly those two books that won the prize. He was a shitty writer before those two books. You want an angle for your story, you find out what happened to him to make him write like that. I have been sitting up here wondering what day it was that he changed from being so self-destructive and faithless into whoever the hell he is now. The work is astounding; more so if you had known him as I did. As my poor sister did. You do your job and find that out, okay?"

Molly watched the tears roll down Meg's cheeks. They were unashamed tears. There was no attempt to dry them or change their course. Molly even saw a tear fall with a ripple into the coffee cup. She knew then that this woman was in love with her subject and that it was a jagged emotion that only came unwrapped rarely.

"I will," Molly promised. The enemy neighbor had enlisted her, but she knew there was no longer a shooting war, only tears.

Roland and Mike had gotten a little lift from the caffeine and whiskey. Roland pressed Mike about the night before, not so much for details, but for observations. The local girls had always fascinated Roland and this Carrie sounded like a fine example of the breed.

"She was a little crusty," said Mike, "but, she was sweet, too. Almost like a naive predator acting mostly on instinct. Actually, she attacked me like a piece of meat, which would have bothered me if I wasn't so sure she would cry if I pushed her away. You know what I mean?"

"Sure do. The sexual revolution was born in Wisconsin bars. If these gals sat around and waited for the men to stop bonding over a football game there would be no proliferation of the species. Men around here don't know how to lead in dancing or sex. Yeah, they are strong women out there in the snow. And good for them and us."

"She was reading your book."

The statement caught Roland off stride. It seemed to cut against his own appraisal of the local women. "She had a copy of *The Tap Root* next to her bed," Mike added.

"Well, that is interesting. Mike, very few people around here read the pop stuff let alone a complicated book like that one. Then of course, I don't know everyone or everything that goes on around here. You read that book, Mike?"

"I picked it up at the airport in Boston. I must admit it is not quite my style, but somebody liked it. The Pulitzer for Christ's sake. Two of them."

Roland was not listening. He was still thinking about the book next to the hot bartender's bed. "Did you read enough to know what it's about?"

"Something about a fat girl."

"Well, yes, I guess that is the minimal plot summary."

"I'm sorry, I just don't read much. I don't really enjoy it."

"No need to apologize. You're a visual guy, hence your work. And you have won every prize for what you do. I haven't failed as a writer if everyone doesn't like my work. I aim at the ones who want to explore a different place inside themselves. In my world the picture is suggested by words. The lens is the human eye. The back of the camera is the brain. The film is the imagination. The final product is emotion. We are not so different, eh?"

"I'll give it another try," said Mike. Roland nodded.

"Let's see if we can find your partner," Roland said as he set his mug down. "We should get this thing started while I am feeling talkative."

The two men left the shed and walked back to the house just as Molly was returning from her walk.

"Where you been, girl?" asked Roland as he put a fatherly arm around her.

Molly moved her chin slightly in the direction she had come from. "I just did a little stroll though your past, Roland."

Roland instantly caught the drift and raised his eyebrows. "Oh shit," he said.

CHAPTER NINE

My writing followed a sort of historical progression as far as tools went. I began to write on yellow legal pads, then moved to an electric typewriter. I was given a word processor as a gift from my first publisher. I supposed at the time that it was a substitute for an advance. I loved it with all my creative heart until the personal computer entered my world. It allowed me to combine the magic of the digital world with the speed required to empty my mind quickly onto the page. In short, it made writing fun and fast. As I became adept, I got my first lap top and had the farm made wireless. This required some doing as we are, of course, off the beaten path for the various cyber-enablers. There is an antenna atop the roof of the house, which somehow connects me to the satellites. This connection I treasure. As a pianist cracks his knuckles before playing his keyboard, I flex my mind skyward toward the silver and gold chariot that enables me to communicate with the world. I could still write on a legal pad, but I would have to somehow have to return to the tools of a cave dweller in order to share them. Now my words can fly as free and fast as the orbit above me allows. I have no sentimental attachment to my past, so why not leap into the future as fast as I can get into it? My life will no doubt end with the closing of a PC note-book lid rather than the lid of a casket.

After breakfast, the first interview session was interrupted by a call to Molly's cell phone from Harry Stompe in Boston. He somewhat bullied Molly into accepting the idea of the girls flying to Wisconsin with his secretary. When Molly suggested that they would only be a distraction to her work, Harry asked to speak to Roland. He took her phone and walked away from her out of the door of the shed where they had decided to work. Molly found herself slightly annoyed that these men were deciding what to do with her children.

When Roland came back in, his cheeks were flush from the cold, but he was smiling. He sat down next to Molly on a couch that was covered with a Navajo blanket. Their knees touched.

"Molly, I know you have reservations about this request of mine, but please be assured it is not some whim of an old, sick man. You must trust me, okay?"

Molly looked at him for a moment in which her brain was ticking off responses. She ultimately came to the only one that made sense. "Okay, I trust you. I hardly know you, but I trust you and Harry. I trust Monica. I trust the freaking friendly skies, for god's sake. I just want this project to work. If having my girls here makes you happy enough to open up to me, then I will trust that will happen. When are they getting here so we can get some work done before the chaos of two very curious little women arrive."

Roland smiled and patted Molly's knee. "Melanie and Sonia should be here in the house by suppertime. They can have the small bedroom upstairs I hope they don't mind sharing a bed."

"All three of us share a bed every time there is a thunderstorm." Molly was going to launch into one last protest, but swallowed it. "You know their names?"

"Of course." He got up and went to a roll top desk and fumbled with some papers. Finding what he was looking for he came back to the couch and handed Molly a computer print out of an article. It included pictures of her and the girls.

"Oh," Molly gasped in recognition. "This is the piece from *The Globe*. This is from three or four years ago when the girls' adoptions were final. It was a nice piece, but I didn't think anyone saw it besides my sister and some of the people at work."

"I am a little embarrassed to tell you, but I did do some research on you before I requested you for this interview and story. I don't want to sound creepy, but it was important to me. I liked something you wrote earlier about a friend of mine, but I wanted to know who you were. The real Molly Costello, as it were."

"Okay, Roland, I will admit I would love to have the girls here. I have never gone on assignment with them. This place has a certain something about it that I think they are going to love. Now, having said all of that can we begin?"

Roland got up and dragged an old overstuffed chair to a spot across a coffee table from where Molly sat. He settled in by crossing his legs and folding his hands behind his head. "Shoot, "he said.

Molly opened her brief case and set her tiny tape recorder on the table between the two of them. Roland looked at it like a cockroach had just leapt on the table. She switched it on, opened a steno pad, and sighed deeply. "Just to break the ice, I have seen at least five pictures of a dog situated around this house. More pictures than of anyone else. Who is he...or she, and why is this dog so prominently displayed?"

"Ah, good question. I knew I was right about you. Her name was Sorry and she was my guide dog when I was blind."

With that preamble, the interview began. The life of Roland Heinz began to pool out into the room like water escaping from behind a dam of many years.

Mike Gabler was keeping himself busy unpacking camera gear in the living room. He had decided to do the portrait shot there because of the western exposure. The lighting was going to be tricky because of the brief window of perfect light that was only available in late afternoon. He was also concerned about the weather cooperating, but figured he would get at least one perfect day and that would be all he needed. The other tricky factor, he figured was Roland himself. He was not going to be a good poser. Mike knew he could snatch the odd candid shot with little problem, but to get him into that chair at the perfect moment would require some cooperation. He decided he would worry about it when the time came.

Mike was also thinking about heading down to the Back Room for his second meeting with Carrie. He sat down for a minute, took in the view, and thought about her. He had used the combination of bars and women for a long time, feeding his compulsion for conquest and companionship. There was a couple girls back in New England that he dated regularly so how could black-eyed Carrie steal his thoughts so fast. He pondered that it might be the foreignness of this part of the upper Midwest. Maybe it was the aggressive way she had moved on him? His mind wandered back to her bed.

Carrie, he mused, was by far the physically strongest woman he had ever known. She was put together pretty well, but it was more than that. Her arms and legs were much more athletic than his. Her lovemaking was in the style of an amateur wrestler. She took him down and pinned him before he could assert any male dominance. Somehow, he liked that and was getting excited just thinking about round two. His smoldering mood was broken by Molly and Roland coming back into the house.

"What have you done to my living room, Mike?" Roland boomed.

"Just unpacking some gear. And you are going to have to sit here for me at some point."

"I've got company coming here in an hour or so and I want this cleaned up. Molly's girls will get into your stuff as sure as shooting."

Molly was all smiles. She had just had a great session with Roland and clutched her tape recorder like a Bible. Normally, she would have someone at the magazine transpose the tape, but that would, of course, be impossible here. She'd need some time alone to listen to it again and begin to write her story. It was an exciting feeling and coupled with the eminent arrival of the girls, she was running on high energy.

Mike and Roland had settled into a conversation about photography so Carrie stole away up to her bedroom. She closed the door and lay down on the bed. It creaked its welcome. She set the recorder next to the pillow and rewound it. Then she let it play back. The voice of Roland Heinz was as soft as her down pillow as he began his narrative:

My wife left me, Carrie, back in '81. It amazes me now that she hung on that long. We were married for fifteen years. I came back from Viet Nam with a variety of problems and, to my regret, I let them simmer. Going to a shrink was never an option back then. Around here it would have been social suicide for it to get out that you were seeing a psychologist. I guess now everyone does, huh? Well, anyway, we had a nice wedding and a tense marriage. I should say right here that we were very much in love before I went into the Army. It was a typical Wisconsin courtship and love affair. I knew her and her family from early on...school and church. I was stuck for a long time between Karin and her sister, Meg. Guess, you kinda heard a little about that today, huh? More on that later.

Anyway, the dog. It was about eight or nine years after Karin left...and I mean left, departed, evaporated. She moved to California, as far away as she could get from me. Found another guy real quick, too, I heard. Anyway, I descended into the culture of the bar and bottle. I drank after work until bar time and beyond. I mostly lit out into the country bars and had a regular route for collecting my daily dosage of anesthesia. This pattern went on for many years and caused most of the health problems I am having now. There's always a price. I wasn't always a writer, of course. I put in about 20 years all together working at one of the local quarries. I am ashamed to say most of that time was a blur. Got my blaster's license and blew up rocks during the day and blew up my liver and marriage every damned night. Because of the noise and chaos at the quarry no one ever knew how hung-over I was or how close I came to screwing up the blasting. Thank goodness my coworkers survived my destructiveness. I sure didn't.

I was writing a little bit in those post marriage days, but it was just crap. I can't even look at that stuff now, but there was a war buddy of mine in Chicago, the C.M. Connell of your past interview. Chick Connell was reading my garbage and came up here a time or two. I think he took pity on me and introduced me to his friend, Harry Stompe, who was a newspaper book reviewer then. Harry hooked me up with a minor publisher who did a limited printing of my first book for a tiny advance, of course. I am getting ahead of myself. Anyway, somewhere along the way I had a crisis. A big one.

One morning I woke up on the porch of a house I did not recognize. It was summer and I was covered with sweat and the corpses of mosquitoes that I must have swatted in my sleep. I didn't feel all that hung-over, but I was creeped out by not knowing where I had landed. The door was open to the house so I looked inside and gave a 'hello.' No answer. I looked outside and saw my old Ford pickup was parked on the lawn. There was a long driveway that led to a country road. Must be somewhere in Calumet County, I figured, but nothing looked even vaguely familiar.

Well, Ms. Costello, to make a long story short, I quickly discovered that I was in Iowa, about ninety miles north of Des Moines. I had no idea how I got there or what had happened along the way. Nothing. I was panicky, to say the least. I drove home all the while fearing that I had left a path of destruction in my wake. I cringed at every cop I passed thinking I would be pulled over and charged with murder or something. I never did find out whose house I had ended up at.

Because of this horrible blackout, I stopped drinking cold turkey. I literally hid inside my house. I was renting a place over in Chilton at the time and no one ever called or checked on me over there. It was the darkest time I had ever known. Karin was gone and so was my ability to forget her on a nightly basis. I could not write a word back then. I might as well have been sealed up in a crypt. Total despair. And then one day a miracle occurred.

I woke up one morning to the sound of barking outside my place. I didn't think much of it at first, but it was persistent. I walked outside and there was this black and white border collie tied to the tree in my front yard. I scratched my head and looked around for an owner. When I went over to look for a tag on the dog's collar, I found a note wrapped in a handkerchief. It simply said, 'I'm an orphan.' I petted the dog and said, 'me, too.' When I took her into the house she acted immediately like she owned the place. Jumped up on the couch and watched me. I said I was sorry I had no dog food and she cocked her head and then...she smiled at me, Molly. I swear to God that dog smiled. I repeated the word 'sorry' and she got up and came to me and put her head in my lap. It was the greatest act of compassion I had ever witnessed. I named her Sorry, but she never made me feel that way. I know there are people who feel that relationships with animals are all in the minds of us humans. That the dog, in this case, was merely being who I wanted her to be for the sake of food and shelter. Some of that is true, but I can tell you without reservation that I loved that dog and she returned every heartbeat of that love. We saw the universes in each other's eyes and were never separated from the first day. I can honestly say that Sorry was the inspiration for me to begin writing in earnest again. It was because of her that my writing changed. I began The Tap Root with her lying at my feet.

Sorry was not a young dog when I found her and she only had the last part of her life to spend with me. She is buried out back by the lilacs where I expect to join her one of these days.

Molly turned off the recorder and decided to take a quick nap. She wondered before she dozed off why, if Roland had a drinking epiphany after his black out, that he was still drinking now. How could he move from problem drinker to social drinker? It defied the accepted logic of what she knew about alcoholism. The subject might not be all that important as it related to his writing, but she was curious. Her own father had died of alcohol related problems. It ran in her family. But, the story of Sorry was good material.

Before she fell into a light sleep she wondered who had tied the dog to the tree outside his house. Did it really matter?

In what seemed like a nano-second later, she awoke to a rap on her door followed by Roland's head popping in. "You awake?"

Molly wasn't sure, but said, "Yeah."

"Just got a call from Monica. They are only about a half hour away. You wanna walk down to the road with me and guide them in?"

Molly sat up and rubbed her eyes, then looked at her watch. "I'll be right down, Roland. Give me a sec."

He closed the door and Molly took a second to get oriented. Then the wave of delight broke over her. The girls were here.

CHAPTER TEN

An owl moved into my barn shortly after my dog died. The bird and I never interacted much except a sort of nodding acknowledgment that it ran the barn and I ran the house and shed. I would see it sometimes with a mouse pinned beneath its talons staring at me. An owl can get under your skin if you let it. In literature they always symbolized death. The Wisconsin barn owl was a wonderful example of the Grim Reaper with wings, somber and well fed with flesh. One day I took a folding chair into the yellow barn with the idea of confronting the bird. It was a September morning, warm, with gauzy sunshine. The barn was dark, but did have some dramatic lighting due to a few holes in the roof. When I sat for a while and my eyes adjusted, there was the owl on a rafter. I am not quite sure how long I sat there and in the presence of my mortality, but the bird never blinked. I did numerous times. I remember noting that summer ended that day and the run up to winter began in my heart. Please do not think that this connection was in any way morbid. The peaceful clock of the universe does not tick. It hums like a tuning fork in a quiet September barn. The bird and I listened together..

Roland, Mike, and Molly walked slowly down to the highway, only slowly because of the ice. They sort of hugged each other in a comic pantomime. It was fun. While they waited for Monica to deliver the girls, Roland gave an abbreviated lecture on the winter constellations. The weather was holding clear and cold and the stars were vivid in the clean, country sky. Molly was interested, but distracted by the approach of each car coming from the south. Mike was mostly interested in that glowing beer sign down the highway to the north. He was going to say his hello's to Molly's kids and then head down the road to see Carrie.

In a short time there was a car coming that was moving slowly as if looking for the turn off. When Roland stepped forward and waved, the car returned his greeting with a honk. Monica pulled just into the driveway and rolled down her window.

"Hello, hello. We're here!"

There were shouts of "Hi Mom!" from the dark interior of the car. Molly ran to the other side and opened the passenger door just as Melanie opened the back door. Sonia hopped out the front into her mom's arms and Melanie almost slipped on the ice trying to do the same.

"Hey, you two little world travelers. I'm so glad to see you!" More hugs.

"I am so glad we don't have to go to school," said Sonia in her cute accent, her brown eyes gleaming. She had her priorities.

"Aunt Monica said you needed us to help you work," said Melanie. Mel was the smart one; Asian Brainchild, Molly called her. She always needed a worthwhile motivation. Helping Mom do her job qualified.

"We can talk about that later. Girls, I want you to meet Mr. Heinz. This is his house we are staying at. Roland was all smiles, as though the girls were a gift delivered to him personally.

"You're the great writer," said Melanie.

"Like Mom," added Sonia.

"Maybe not as good as Mom," said Roland. "Welcome to Ghost Farm girls."

The girls looked at each other with wide eyes and then turned to Molly and said in unison, "Ghosts?"

"Maybe a few," Molly joshed. "Sonia, Melanie, this is Mike Gabler. He's a great photographer."

"Hi," said Mike as he stepped forward. "We are all great people here. You guys will fit in just fine."

The girls shied up and blushed. Mike had a way with ladies of all ages, it seemed.

"Well, com'on everyone. Let's get up to the house and have something to eat. Everyone is hungry right?" said Roland.

The girls nodded.

"Monica," he added, "I think you can make it up the hill if you take it slow. We'll walk and meet you up there." He then leaned in close to her window and whispered to her, "Thank you so much for doing all this."

"It was my pleasure, Mr. Heinz," said Monica. "The girls are dolls and great traveling companions."

"We can talk about getting you home in the morning, dear. Got a nice bed for you tonight."

"Great. I'm exhausted."

As Monica began to negotiate the drive, Molly waited for a second and looked at Mike. He gave her a little shrug and wave. She expected him to leave. When she turned to head to the house she noticed that Sonia and Melanie were holding Roland's hands. They were both normally shy about meeting new people, but they looked so natural with Roland. She heard them laughing at something he said and a kind of soft feeling like an old family memory came over her. She looked at the stars again for an instant and then followed the group up hill.

As the main group headed up to the farm house, Mike took his leave and headed for The Back Room. It was his bed that Monica was getting whether he repeated his night at Carrie's place or not. He hadn't so much as dented the pillow at the farm house yet and really didn't care to. He would worry about finding a couch later if things were chilly with Carrie. His ego said not to worry, but some voice in his head reminded him that he was in a foreign land amongst unpredictable natives. He pondered all of this as he crunched down the shoulder of Highway 151. It was a treacherous walk, especially when an oncoming car came by. The footing was a bit tricky at the bar too, when he finally got there.

Carrie nodded to Mike when he walked in and took his lucky stool from the night before. She nodded, but did not rush over, which he took mental note of. A good minute went by before she gave the old bar rag a toss over the shoulder and ambled down. Mike knew this was not going to be the same rules as before. He had played this game long enough to know that the rules rarely remained constant. He waited patiently for her to break the ice.

"Hi." was all he got so he returned the serve.

"Hi." Stalemate. He waited. She waited.

"Bah-Kaadi coke?"

"I think I'll have a glass of Miller Lite and a kind word, bartender."

Carrie drew the beer from the closest tap and set it down in front of him.

"Here's your beer and the kind word is..."

"Is what?"

"Oh, hell, I don't know, Mike. I was trying to be cool and it never works"

"Never?"

"Don't press it."

"How was your day?"

And so the small talk continued until someone down the bar needed a refill. All Mike could think was that he really liked her. The off center approach of hers was a classic move and perfect for the situation. She was watching him, too. Another good sign. At least it was, until the sound of snowmobile engines roared outside the bar. Mike looked over his shoulder and saw headlights outside. He looked back at Carrie and saw concern in her eyes. He knew the story about the cat fight, the rogue sledders and immediately felt his own anxiety. Was there a chance that he was going to have to step in and help Carrie? He was a lover, not a fighter.

There were two couples and for some reason they sat down at Mike's end of the bar. And yes, he noted, one of the women had a knot on her forehead the size and shape of a jumbo egg. The snowmobilers stomped their boots and began unzipping some of the heavy riding clothing. It looked to Mike like they were making camp. Suddenly he felt like he was in a wild west saloon with trouble brewing. Carrie came down and faced her old foe.

"How's your head? Mine still hurts," Carrie began.

The woman with the knob seemed hesitant. "It's getting better."

One of the men, a big bearded guy soft punched the woman. "Com'on, Deb, say your piece."

The woman named Deb glared at the guy, but then turned to Carrie. "I came here to apologize for the other night. I was shit-faced and out of line."

Mike, who had a mouthful of beer almost choked. He had been chugging his beer for courage and never expected the apology.

"Yeah, I know how it goes when you bar hop cross county. I'll accept your apology if you let me buy all of you a round. You need some ice for that thing?" Carrie made a funny face that disarmed everyone. The group got their free drinks, slammed them, and headed back out into the cold to the next bar down the snowmobile trail. Mike got them to pose for a group picture with Carrie before they departed. Years later he still treasured that picture and the story that went along with it.

At bar time, which was an early 12:45AM on this week night, Carrie was doing the closing ritual while Mike waited to see what was going to happen. When she was done with everything but the lights and lock, she came to him.

"You gonna walk me home?"

Mike smiled and nodded. He saw a different look in her eye that the night before. The lust was gone, replaced by something more innocent yet more appealing. They walked silently across the street and stopped at her back door.

"You wanna go for a little walk," she said, still holding his hand. They were not wearing gloves and their hands seemed welded to one another.

"I think I would like that," Mike said softly. They turned away from the doorway and its warm promise and headed east across the snowfield. There was a path of sorts. It was several minutes before Carrie broke the silence.

"You're being here has something to do with Roland Heinz, right?"

"How did you figure that out? Oh, never mind, it's no secret. Yeah, I am doing the photos for a story that someone is writing about him."

"How long will you be around here, Mike?"

"Maybe a week or so... Actually, it can't be longer than that. I have another shoot back in Massachusetts."

They walked a little farther in silence.

"Have you read any of his books?" Carrie asked.

"I started one of them, uh, *The Tap Root*. I am having trouble getting into it so far."

"My mom gave it to me and I can't put it down. I have never read anything like it. I love it."

"Tell me about it, Carrie."

She gave his had a squeeze, probably because she had never had a literary discussion in her life, let alone with some guy she had picked up and slept with the night before. The squeeze was an involuntary flex of her fingers connected to her heart.

"Well, it's about this girl who is morbidly obese. You know, like really overweight. It follows her through the last three days of her life."

"Sounds depressing."

"You would think so when you start it, but no, it is very uplifting. Spiritual. The story reads like ...I don't know, maybe a poem. Her dreams are a lot like mine, in fact. She is really a beautiful person."

"So how does she die?"

"Hah, you have to read the book." With that statement she turned to Mike and kissed him. It was a different kiss than the hot, wet ones the night before. This one had her lips telling him a story. There was something about the cold air and the smell of her hair that was adding to the effect and in that moment the entire world shrunk into the space occupied by the two of them. He knew they were not going to bed together that night and suddenly he didn't care. He just wanted to stay in that snowy field and kiss her all night.

Sonia woke up in the middle of the night and nudged Molly. "Where's the bathroom, Mom?" The girls had decided to sleep with their mom in the strange house that might have ghosts.

"Ssh, I'll show you," Molly whispered. "Don't wake up your sister."

"I'm wake," said Melanie matter-of-factly. "I gotta go, too."

"Okay, girls follow me." The three of them poured out of the big bed and went out into the hall. While the girls were taking care of their business, Molly saw a light on downstairs and heard a throat clear. She walked down three steps and peeked into the living room. Mike was laying down on the couch with a blanket over him, reading by the light of a stately floor lamp.

"You okay down here, Mike?"

He looked up from his book and over the top of reading glasses. "Yeah, Molly, just fine."

She walked down a couple more steps, aware that she was in her flannel pajamas. "I thought you'd be out all night, Romeo." There was a small, good-natured barb in her statement.

"Naw," sighed Mike, setting the book down on his chest. "Even satyrs need the occasional night off."

"I see you're reading Roland's book. Thought you said it didn't interest you."

Mike took off his reading glasses and smiled at Molly. He could now see the feet of the two girls a couple steps above her. "Let's just say it was assigned reading."

"Huh?"

"You'd better get those Munchkins back to bed."

Molly looked up the stairs and then nodded at Mike and waved a goodnight.

He thought about snapping off the light, but instead picked the book back up. He wanted to read about Carrie's dreams.

CHAPTER ELEVEN

My favorite moments in the creation of a book are composing the very first and very last words. I have never compared notes on this with other writers, so I do not know if I stand alone here. The act of striking the keys that produce that initial word is an act of courage. It is the headfirst dive into the deep end of the pool without having first checked the temperature of the water or its actual depth. The last word, when finally written, is the confirmation that you have come back up to the surface and the air is again filling your lungs. So, you see, the story is written at the bottom of the pool. You are holding your breath. You are kicking your feet. The pressure is squeezing your head. Your characters begin to school like fish around you. They live within the time limit of your lung capacity. It is alien and frantic. It is also embryonic. Amniotic. Aquatic. Erotic. In the end you gasp, pull your self out of the pool, and immediately head for the diving board once more. Writing is the only addiction I ever acquired that I never even intended to escape. And I had a bunch of them.

The next day's session of interviewing began immediately after Monica's departure and kept Molly and Roland in the studio from breakfast until their late lunch. Mike had kept Sonia and Melanie entertained by showing them some camera tricks. They had gone for a walk around the property and he let the girls experiment with his small digital camera. It was obvious to Molly at lunch that some bonding had taken place as the girls gabbled constantly about 'Mike this and Mike that.' She was relieved and pleased that the girls were not moping around, whining about being bored. After all, Roland did not have a television, the universal babysitter. Instead they put on a slide show on Mike's laptop of their day in the field. It was funny, entertaining, and also featured some interesting photography.

Mom's morning session had also been productive and she now felt she had a grip on Roland's early years. By his own telling, his life was not uncommon for a man of his era growing up in this area. As she looked at her notes later, she was reminded of Meg Bollander's clue: look for the incident or circumstance that caused his writing to change so quickly from mediocre to brilliant. Molly knew she was getting closer to that time and looked forward to the next day's interview. She knew it was linked to finding the dog in the yard, but something else must have happened. Since *The Tap Root* was the breakout work, she wondered who was the inspiration for Garnet Granger, the strange, obese heroine. She quickly made some additional notes for herself. Roland found her at the kitchen table.

"I hope you don't mind, we're taking tomorrow off," he stated.

"Oh?"

"I have a doctor's appointment," Roland said with a sheepish smile. "It won't take long, but there is some prep time involved and I will probably lose focus for a while as far as you go."

Molly saw an opening she had been avoiding until now. "Roland, am I allowed to ask about your health?"

Roland nodded in a benign way. "There is nothing off limits to you, Molly."

"So, what's going on, Roland? Are you okay?"

This time Roland let go a genuine laugh. "My dear, I am a ticking time bomb medically, but yes, everything is okay. You could say we all suffer from terminal nativity. We are born to die, but if we are lucky enough to get the time here to do our work, then it is nothing to mope about. I am going to my oncologist tomorrow. He will, no doubt, tell me what I already know and collect his rather large fee from my insurance company. He will get richer and I will get a day older."

"How bad is your cancer?"

Roland sighed deeply. "I am told it is pretty nonaggressive, slow moving. In a race between my heart and my cancer killing me, bet on the heart."

Molly drank this information in and mulled it over. What could she say next? Before she could come up with something, he sensed her confusion and changed the subject.

"Molly, why don't you introduce the girls to Meg tomorrow. Set up a lunch. I am sure she would love the chance to get out of her routine of sitting up there loathing me. And when I say that, it is without sarcasm. She has her rights. But, she is a good woman, as you know, and getting her side of our story might be interesting before you get mine. We'll talk about my wife the next time and I can't do that without talking about Meg.

"You really are fearless, aren't you?"

"Well, if you mean the health issues, maybe more philosophical than brave. But, when it comes to the Bollander girls, I am scared to freaking death."

Molly smiled. "Okay, I'll call her. What are we doing the rest of the day?"

"I am going to let Mike do his portrait. I think he is getting distracted by one of our local girls and needs to get back to work."

Molly, of course, had noticed Mike's distraction, too. The reporter in her wanted to meet this mystery woman. Also, she was feeling a little jealous. Mike had sort of flirted with her from their first encounter and, while she didn't think he was her type, she missed the attention. "Do you know who this lady is?"

"I know she works down at the local bar and I know she is reading one of my books. Those two facts are rather oxymoronic."

"Oh?"

"Almost no one around here knows who I am are what I do...or cares. If a story is not on film, it doesn't sell. Your magazine would not sell a single copy in this part of the world."

"I'll mention that to Harry. He likes a challenge."

"Hah, that's one arrow he could shoot into the air that would never come back down. Hey, for all I know, the lack of literary interest here may be what pushed me to write. I was not distracted by other local writers getting attention from the press. The climate was a vacuum that I filled. Right place, right time."

"You certainly have interesting insights into things, Roland."

He smiled and winked. "It's a gift!"

Molly placed a call to Meg to try to set up a lunch for the next day, but only got the answering machine so she decided to take the girls into town to do some shopping. She needed more micro-cassettes for her recorder and the girls needed some warmer outdoor clothes. She took the rental van and headed into Fond du Lac to the mall. It was difficult to drag Sonia and Melanie past Mike's photo set up in the living room as the girls were fascinated not only with all things camera, but all things Mike. Eventually she got them out of the house, leaving Roland and Mike to their session.

Mike had a certain vision of what he wanted from this portrait. The clear weather was going to deliver the lighting he wanted in a couple hours, but he was going to have to make Roland jump through some wardrobe hoops and knew that would be problematic. This was going to be the cover shot, the money-maker. Reputations were made on these highly visible advertisements of the photographer's talent. *Art Harvest* was not in the front racks like *Time, Newsweek*, or *People*, but it was read by many of Mike's peers and that mattered a lot to him.

"How's this look?" asked Roland as he stepped into the living room. He was dressed in dark slacks with a gray crew-neck sweater and a white shirt beneath it. Mike studied him and frowned.

"No good, huh?"

"Actually, you look very nice, Roland, but this is not what I am looking for. Let's go look in your closet."

"Ain't much in there...maybe some skeletons."

"Let's look, anyway." They went upstairs.

Mike found a coat very close to what he was looking for. A gray corduroy jacket that was a little frayed around the cuffs. He decided he wanted Roland in blue jeans, but didn't see any.

"You got any jeans, Roland?"

Roland smiled. "I got some, but we don't hang them up in the closet like you Easterners. No presses or creases in our jeans around here." He went to a chest of drawers and pulled out several pairs of denim pants and laid them on the bed. Mike looked them over.

"Everything fits?"

"Maybe a little baggy now. I've lost some weight due to the cancer, I suppose."

The mention of the cancer caused Mike to mentally flinch. He didn't say anything, but kept handling the jeans. It was Molly's job to get the story, he reminded himself. He already loved Roland as a friend, but he was a very new friend; not someone he could get that personal with.

"Okay, I like these if they fit. This dark blue shirt is nice with the coat."

"Those jeans have a hammer loop on the side. That okay?"

"That, Roland, is perfect. Get dressed and we can start to light you."

The mall in town was small compared to the great suburban malls around Boston, but it was functional for the shopping Molly needed. The girls each got sweaters and new boots that were well suited to trudging around Ghost Farm in the cold. In the checkout lines the other shoppers were small-talking about the weather and how a big snow was coming in over night. This excited the kids, but made Molly a little nervous. Getting snowed in was okay up to a point, but she wondered how it would affect Roland. Would bad weather distract him or impact his health issues. In a moment of contemplation, Molly realized that it was her own deep fears that made her anxious about the coming storm. Her parents had died in a snow storm when a truck jackknifed on the interstate near Barnstable in '87 and crossed over the highway. They were coming to visit her at the time so guilt combined with bad weather haunted her. She was distracted at the cashier by these thoughts to the extent that someone behind her had to nudge her. She snapped to and thought is was rude until she turned around and saw the grinning face of Meg Bollander.

"Wake up, Molly. No day-dreaming in line on a sale day."

The girls were astounded that anyone local knew their mom. They could only stare at Meg.

"Why, hello Meg. This is such a coincidence. I tried to call you earlier," said Molly.

"And these are your daughters?" Meg asked, while putting her hand on Melanie's shoulder.

"Yes, this is Melanie and this is Sonia."

"Hi. Welcome to Wisconsin, girls."

The girls looked back to their mom for guidance.

"Say hi to Mrs. Bollander, girls"

Sonia was the smartass of the pair. "Hello to Mrs. Bollander girls," she dead-panned. Melanie punched her arm, which caused a punch back.

"As you can see, Meg, they are barbarians."

"They will get along fine with the local stock, I think. So, why did you call me, Molly?"

"Roland has a doctor's appointment tomorrow and he suggested we do lunch."

The mere mention of Roland's name cause Meg's eyebrow's to rise reflexively. "Well, perhaps we should obey the great man's orders, but we can do it today instead of tomorrow. Besides, I'm hungry. You girls hungry?"

They girls both nodded. Ten minutes later they were seated in a booth at the Applebee's adjacent to the mall. Melanie and Sonia were content to color their placemats and critique each other's art work. Molly and Meg sat on the outside with their heads leaning in close as though conspiring.

"He told me to get your side of the story first," whispered Molly.

"Hmm, shrewd tactic. I talk first and he can pick my story apart without me being present for the cross examination," Meg said, not whispering at all.

Molly checked to see that the girls had no interest in what they were saying. "Can you give me the PG version? Our next session is going to be about your sister. His words were something like I should hear it from you first. Her name was Karin, right?"

The food arrived just then and the mood was broken.

"Tell you what," said Meg, "let's meet later and do this. I think it might do me some good to tell the story to a relative stranger. What you want to use out of it is your call. I don't want to have to mince my words for them." She meant the girls. Molly nodded.

"Where do you want to meet? I think it is going to snow later."

"There is a happy hour at the bar on 151. The Back Room. I will pick you up at the end of Roland's drive at 5 o'clock with my ATV. A little snow is no problem around here."

"Can you drive that on the roads?"

"We'll be driving in the ditch. Same as the road this time of year. Date?"

"Date."

Sonia looked up suddenly. "Mom's got a date!"

Melanie who didn't look like she was paying attention said, "She has a date with Meg, Sony, so they don't have to talk about Roland in front of us."

Meg looked at the girls and let go a low chuckle. "I love you two already." She reached for the check, but Molly was quicker.

"Expense account," said Molly.

"Good," said Meg.

There was a halo around the late afternoon sun, an omen of the snow to come, but Mike never noticed it as he did his last minute tweaking for Roland's portrait.

"Am I going to blow a fuse, when these strobes fire?"

"I don't know, Mike. I sit in the dark mostly, don't use much electricity," Roland answered.

"Well, I know these old farmhouses can be tricky. I am using the smallest flashes I could carry for this job, but they do suck a lot of juice for a quick second. I am almost afraid to test them."

"What happens if they blow the fuse?"

"I am using them as filler light on the part of you that is not facing the sun coming in the window. I'm thinking I will only have about five good minutes to do this. But, even if the fuse blows I should get something. I will need to read the light meter constantly, which is something my camera assistant would normally be doing. I was going to use Molly, but maybe it is better with just you and me. You ready, Roland. The light is beginning to work."

Roland sat in a wooden captain's chair dressed in his chosen wardrobe. The look was 'country writer.' Mike had done the best he could on his own with the wardrobe, hair, etc. and now it was show time. The sun had dropped just below the top of the picture window looking west. The sun was angling in from the southwest and the widow was beginning to frame it. He decided to let the angle work for him that way. When the time was right there would be a little shadow on Roland's nose and down his lips and chin. Mike knew the eyes would light up, too, but didn't know exactly how that would work. The background was knotty pine, which he thought was perfect.

One thing that was certain was that he was going to have to work fast. There were two cameras set on tripods to give him two different angles. The expensive digital hung around his neck. He had planned his moves for the last two hours; how he would dance between the cameras, both of which were synched to the strobes. One shot color film and the other would shoot black and white. He knew there would be no time to change film in the tripod cameras so he would need to fire them like machine guns and pray he got the shot. He didn't want to have to do this again and he knew Roland didn't either.

As the sun burst into the room the frantic activity began for Mike. Roland sat patiently and reacted to the subtle commands for movement. They had already agreed there would be no smiles, but as things got going, Roland found it almost comical. He did restrain himself, however.

Mike began with a burst of digital shots as the sun hit Roland's face. He then shot about half of the color roll without the strobe. He then emptied the camera with the strobe. The house fuse held. He ran to Roland and made some adjustments to the wardrobe and then ran back to the black and white camera. This one really needed the strobe and, of course, the fuse blew after about ten rapid fire trips of the shutter. He continued to empty the camera anyway.

The light was now sprinting down the wall and would be off Roland's face in a minute or two. Mike went to the digital around his neck and darted around the room looking for that certain something that was his trademark. Nearing the last possible second of perfect sunlight a bright flash blasted into the room. Mike had no time to either curse or adjust, but he knew instinctively that it was the reflection off of Molly's windshield as she turned into the drive. It was only an instant and he knew it wouldn't ruin anything, but the intrusion of Molly and the girls would. He finished just as the front door burst open and the girls came in.

"Wow!" exclaimed Sonia, admiring all the equipment.

"Oh, sorry," said Molly. "Should we go back outside?"

"No come on in," said Mike. "We just finished. Mr. Heinz, that's a wrap."

"Wrap?" said Melanie. She was looking at all the cords and cameras. "You mean we missed it?"

"You only missed the hard part, Mel," Mike chirped. "We can look at the pictures together later, okay?"

Melanie nodded. Molly sent them upstairs with their packages so she could have a word with the men.

"Everything go okay, Mike?"

"I think so. We blew a fuse with the strobes, but I think I may have gotten what I want."

"What do you think, Roland?" Molly asked. She was digesting his wardrobe with the hammer loop and frayed cuffs on the old coat. She had a mental flash that she should trust Mike.

"I think it was interesting and most important it's finished," Roland said as he got up stiffly from the chair. "Never seen a man move so fast as Mike here."

"The light, Roland, the light," Mike injected.

For a second they all turned toward the sun as it dipped below the Lake Winnebago horizon. It was magical and Mike took the moment to take a couple pictures of Molly.

"What's that for?" she asked. She had the usual female love-hate thing for having her picture taken spontaneously.

"It just caught my eye. You looked very lovely just then."

"Oh, just then?" She pushed Mike's upper arm and giggled. "Hey, that reminds me, I have a date."

Both men locked their attention on her. She enjoyed the suspense she had created.

"I am meeting Meg at 5 o'clock. I need a babysitter."

The men looked at one another. Mike spoke up first. "Um, I sort of had something to do later myself."

Mike and Molly turned to Roland. "Well, if I am going to get skewered by you women and ditched by Mike, I guess that leaves me and the girls. Not a problem. I have all your cell phone numbers on speed dial already, anyway. You may both go in peace."

Molly walked down the drive at precisely 5pm and found Meg already waiting for her. She hopped on the ATV and they made the short trip down to the Back Room in less than one minute. Soon they were huddled at a back table over Molly's Old Fashion and Meg's Kessler's and water. Molly was watching the lady bartender very closely.

"I suppose she is the one that has my photographer in a tizzy," snipped Molly. She instantly didn't like the way it came out. "Actually, she is very pretty."

"That's Pat and Tom Stirling's daughter. Think her name is Carrie. She's been here a long time for such a pretty girl," Meg noted. "The pretty ones usually get out as soon as they can. Move away to California or some place warm."

"But, you stayed."

"Hah, I should have left way back when. I'da made a good hippie chick in San Francisco or something like that. I was a free spirit. Much more so than my sister, which leads us nicely onto our topic for the evening." Meg swirled her drink and took a large gulp. She sucked on an ice cube waiting for Molly to begin.

Molly took her micro-recorder out of her purse and set it on the table. "You mind?"

"As a matter of fact, I do, dear. I don't want any of this coming back to me."

"So we are off the record tonight?"

"Yes, very much so." Meg noticed Molly's mouth turn down. "Hey, I am going to be honest with you and you can ask me anything, but use it as background, okay? My past concerning your subject is complicated and I could say the wrong thing to you. Especially after a few of these."

"You're right, of course. I am not here to do an article on you."

"Right."

"Okay so let's just do a little girl talk."

Carrie came by and the two women each ordered another drink. When they were delivered, the conversation began. Molly let Meg lead the way.

"I was always protective of my little sister, Karin. She was a little doll; by far the prettiest girl in the county. Every guy was interested in her. I didn't mind because it meant I got lots of attention, too. "

"I have a sister like that, too."

"So you know. Well, anyway, Roland Heinz was the best looking boy around and we all were after his attention. Everyone, but Karin. She liked some other guy back then, but I thought Roland had a thing for her. When it turned out he was after me I was stunned...but not so stunned that I couldn't picture the wedding at the Elks Club, the polka band, the honeymoon, the kids, the long and happy life together. Back in those days when you found your guy you sealed the deal early, if you know what I mean."

"You slept with him."

"You had sex and actually hoped for a pregnancy. We were all horny Catholic girls and there was no contraception. Get the guy hooked; that was the plan. Mr. Heinz and I did it every place and every which way from Sunday."

"But, no pregnancy?"

Meg shook her head with the same vehemence she had felt most of her life. Molly noticed there was a plea in her eyes, as though she might have the answer to a question posed fifty some years ago. "But, surely he didn't lose interest in you because you guys didn't have a baby?"

"No, not precisely, but it gave him time to get to know Karin. When he came over to see me, she hung around. We even double dated quite often. Somehow, it was during one of those double dates that we sort of exchanged affections. We had dropped her date off and the three of us were in the front seat of Roland's car. I was in the middle, of course, fiddling with the radio. When I leaned back I felt something funny across my back. It was their arms. Molly, they were holding hands behind my back. Oh, they broke it off real quick and sly, but I knew. My God, if I had caught them fucking in the cornfield I would not have been as wounded as catching them in that simple act of love. Holding hands, sweet Jesus, I was jealous and turned away from both of them. Not all at once, but slowly, subtly."

"Surely, you can look back and see that as something, what, innocent, Meg?"

"I loved them both, Molly. I was angry and rejected, but I loved them both. It was later that I came to loath Roland. It was after their wedding that I actually danced at. It was when he came back from the war that he murdered my sister's love and the ghost of mine. It's what he did to her, the little sister I always protected. Goddamn it, I need another drink!"

CHAPTER TWELVE

I sometimes wonder how many great books are never read by anyone, save the author and a few chosen friends and family. Children who are avid readers often try their luck with writing at some point with various degrees of stamina. Once you have written to even the smallest acclaim you begin to realize that there is a promised land out there that you are probably never going to reach. The simple word 'published' means much more to a writer than even the words 'forgiveness' or 'salvation." It means everything. A man or woman can hammer down the gates guarding access to success to almost any other career other than a literary one. One can even become the St. Peter of this realm and become a publisher. Or one of its angels, the editor. But, the keys to this kingdom require three difficult elements and they may never vary: talent, luck, and access. Two of the three will never work because they all begin to wind around each other from the first written word. From the inside, having been published and awarded prizes and money for my work, I still look back through the window I passed through and see the loneliness of books without covers. They sit in boxes and on shelves waiting for mildew and mice to put them out of their silent misery. Forgotten writers, I still walk with you.

Mike Gabler was purposely slow putting away his gear. He knew Molly was meeting Meg down at the Back Room and was not eager to put his pursuit of Carrie on display, especially for Molly. He knew she thought she had him figured out and didn't want to prove her right even if she was. Besides, he mused, there is an art to courting a bartender that required concentration and an openness to improvisation. An audience cramped his style. It always had.

As Mike puttered with his cases, Roland was entertaining the girls in the kitchen. In order to compete with Mike for their attention he had set up a writing workshop at the kitchen table. He had supplied Melanie and Sonia with paper and pencil and was urging them to make up a story.

"Okay, girls, here's how we do it. Melanie, you write a sentence and then pass the paper to Sonia who will continue the story. Then it will be my turn and then around the table until we finish.

"What should I write? I don't know how to start," Melanie whined. This was supposed to be a vacation from school and knowing Mike was in the next room with his cameras was making her feel trapped.

Roland, of course, knew this. "Start with once upon a time and then go from there."

"Okay, once upon a time," Melanie spoke as she wrote. "There was a beautiful princess who was being kept against her will in the kitchen of an..."

"Old ogre?" Roland inserted.

Sonia laughed and then asked, "What's an ogre?" Melanie was embarrassed.

"I wasn't going to say that."

"I know, dear, but I said it so it goes in the story. Your turn Sonia. And he repeated the line.

Sonia thought hard and then said with great drama in her voice, "And the beautiful princess was really in love with the handsome prince in the living room."

Melanie threw her pencil at Sonia and Roland had to intervene. "Okay ladies, you write down what ever comes into your head while I make some hot chocolate. The handsome prince needs to work alone and we are helping him by staying out of his royal way."

Melanie followed Roland to the stove and helped him get the mugs down and put tiny marshmallows into them. Sonia somehow got inspired and began to write furiously.

The Ledge

When he could do it without becoming obvious, he would watch the young Vietnamese girl. What Melanie and her country meant to him was requiring great thought on his part. He was thinking that she, in some way, might represent a happy ending to his long and personal war. She could be the grandchild of either an enemy or an ally, but it didn't really matter which one. She was the perfect flower that grew from a scorched landscape; the symbol of a rebirth that he had never visualized or sensed. That a child of Vietnam could be helping him make hot chocolate in his own kitchen in Wisconsin all these years later, was doing what no shrink could ever have done with mere words. In that moment she leaned against him and stirred the hot milk. He knew then she had been sent there as an agent carrying a message he longed to hear.

When Roland looked over at Sonia, her brown hands gripping her pencil like a life line, he saw another sight that made his heart do a good kind of beat-skipping. The little child of Africa was writing a story at his table, as though he had passed a family trait on to her.

"Is the milk supposed to bubble, Papa?'

"What?" Roland was not sure he had heard what Melanie had called him. "What did you call me, Mel?"

"Papa. Is that okay? You are like my grandfather, right, and I will call you Papa."

Before Roland could say a word Sonia chimed in.

"Come read my story, Papa."

The rest of the evening was beyond his words.

When Molly came home to relieve Roland, Mike was just about to leave the house. He stopped to chat with Molly for a minute before he left.

"How did go down there? Get some good stuff?"

"I got some stuff. Mrs. Bollander is a pretty neat lady."

"But, she hates him?" Mike nodded towards the kitchen where they could hear the girls and Roland talking softly.

"Yes, but it's not exactly that simple. She actually has been in love with him for most of her life. And speaking of which." Meg paused for effect. "I met your girlfriend."

"Well, she's not exactly..."

"Yeah, I know." Molly interrupted. "She's a doll.

"You jealous, Molly?" Mike had intoned it so it sounded like a joke and she got it.

"Sure I am. My photographer loves my bartender. My kids love you and Roland. "Meg loves Roland, too. So who the hell loves me?"

Mike put on his jacket and gloves and opened the door. "We all love you Molly Costello. The question is, in the words of the late, great Bo Diddley, 'who do you love?" With that he was out the door. Molly stood there and considered a deep sigh, but swallowed it and went into the kitchen.

When Mike saw a white stretch limo parked and idling on the side of the Back Room he was curious. It seemed so out of place in Pipe. Inside, Carrie was behind the bar, but there was a group of locals gathered around the far end who seemed to be celebrating something or other. The laughter and shouting was way beyond the normal low hum of rustic drinking and he noticed that Carrie didn't look too happy. He parked in his usual spot by the door and waited patiently; and then impatiently. He didn't want service so much as he wanted Carrie. Eventually, she shot him a glance and he could tell from her eye language that it was the first time she saw him. Something or someone down there in the huddle at the other end of the bar was keeping her from moving away.

A quick option for leaving immediately leapt into Mike's head, but he decided to wait it out. Carrie looked a little distressed. Again she glanced at him with a pained look now as if begging his patience. He decided to swivel his view to the window and watch the snow, which had begun to fall in rather large flakes. For some reason he could not get the Bo Diddley song out of his mind. It was playing over and over again. Bo used his guitar for rhythm and percussion and it had Mike nodding his head. *Who do you love, who do you love?*

Somewhere between the snowflakes and the song Carrie tapped him on the shoulder. "I am so sorry, Mike."

Mike swiveled back around and expected a bright smile, but saw a dark frown. Her pretty eyebrows were knit. "What's wrong? You look vexed."

"I am vexed. I can't believe this shit is happening here."

Mike shot a glance down the bar. "Got problems down there?"

"You could say that. My, um... ex just showed up and, as usual, he's causing a stir."

"Your ex?" Mentally, Mike was thinking, well at least he's an ex.

"Yeah, maybe you've heard of him. Crazy Ray Hitowski."

Mike looked at Carrie with his eyebrows halfway up his forehead. Then he looked down the bar and saw the unmistakable face. A face he knew quite well, actually.

"Oh shit, you're not going to like this, Carrie, but I have had photo sessions with Ray and his band two or three times. We actually know each other...pretty well." The last statement was followed by a nervous laugh. Molly was clearly stricken and not laughing. The bar rag came up over her shoulder, a sure sign of trouble and she stomped back down to the other end of the bar.

Mike watched as she said something to Ray and saw him look down. Mike gave a weak wave, which got Ray up and strutting over to him. Crazy Ray was the archetypical aging rocker, earrings, tats, pony tail, and a build like Iggy Pop.

"Holy shit. As I live and breathe! What the fuck are you doing in these parts, Mike? Man, you just never fuckin' know, huh?" Ray grabbed Mike's hand and wrung hard, then threw it off. "You working around here or what, man?"

Mike wanted to tell Ray he was fucking his ex, but restrained himself. "I am doing a photo shoot on a local writer. Only been here a couple days. I knew you were from Wisconsin, but well, small world and all that."

"Fucking minuscule, man."

"So what are you doing here, Ray?"

"Something I should have done years ago. I am going to get a divorce from that cunt." He thumb jerked in Carrie's direction.

The use of the 'c-word' was a true character definer for Mike. Men who used it were the lowest of the low. The fact that it had been used to describe Carrie brought his blood to the boiling point. Instantly. A fast burn. Mike then did a couple things that were calculated in less than second. First, he sized up Crazy Ray. He decided he could take him. Then he summoned some courage to match his rage. Then he hauled off and pole-axed the little bandy rooster with a snap right jab. Ray's lights went out immediately and Mike stood over him with the dual devils of pride and remorse sitting on his shoulders. The bar went dead silent for a second. Then there were shouts and angry people running at him. He was tackled and dragged down by a couple of Ray's posse mates and Mike instinctively curled into a fetal position to fend off any blows or kicks. The next thing he knew Carrie was pushing the guys off him and screaming that the cops were coming.

"Good," said one guy. "I saw this guy swing first. Assault and battery."

"You wanna stay here?" screamed Carrie, "Fine." With that she reached into the still dazed Ray's jacket pocket and pulled out a rather long brown tube containing some white powder. The two guys looked at the drug jug like vampires look at a crucifix.

"Fuck, you put that on him," said the another posse guy.

"You wanna play that game with the local cops, asshole? Stick around. I'll buy you guys a beer."

Both of Ray's buddies looked at each other and then, seeing the twisted wisdom in Carrie's words, lifted Crazy Ray up and got him moving to the limo. Mike was on his feet in time to watch them drive off into the snow. When he turned around to Carrie she gave him a hard push.

"What did you do that for? Jesus Christ, Mike!"

Mike smoothed his hair back and took a deep breath. It had been a strange few minutes. Now he was pissed off, too. "He called you a name. The worst name."

"He called me a name? Who the fuck cares what he calls me?'

Mike looked at Carrie. He saw the anger in her eyes and he knew he could never imagine the amount of time that it took to set it there so deeply. He realized he had walked in on something that he had no business becoming a part of. He grabbed his jacket and went to the door.

"I care," he said and left the bar.

He half-expected to be side swiped by the limo on his way down the highway back to Roland's place. If it happened, he didn't really care about that.

CHAPTER THIRTEEN

I purchased Ghost Farm with book money. I got it pretty cheap as sanctuaries go. Who could ever put a price on a peaceful refuge; the place where you would make the transition between all the things that were important when you were young to the place where you hoped time would stand still in your old age. I had never bought property outright before and had to have my hand held by Realtors and lawyers all the way. The day I got the keys and walked into my kitchen with Sorry was amazing. I remember her sniffing around and quickly finding an old couch to her liking. She was not happy when I had the place cleaned and decorated, something it needed badly. Fortunately, she seemed to prefer new leather to musty cloth furniture. I kept the bedrooms as they had been left by the previous owners. I think dairy farmers really knew how to sleep. While the old owners would not recognize the lower part of the house or their cheese shed, they would find that time has stood still upstairs. I sometimes dream about them dreaming. I hear a branch rub against the wall and think of them hearing it years ago. There are creaks in the floor near the bathroom that they must have heard when they got up in the night. I think I hear their voices sometimes, but it is probably only the wind and the house. But, then what is a ghost, but the wind and an old house?

The next morning was Wednesday. As soon as Roland left for his doctor's appointment Molly called Meg and she came down to the farm on her ATV. She, of course, would not come inside. She had agreed to take the girls for a couple hours so that Molly and Mike could make a quick call back to Boston and try to figure out where they were pertaining to the project. They had not really been alone since the drive up from the airport in Milwaukee in what seem like light years ago. Mike took a picture of the girls and Meg as they drove off hugging each other aboard the little four-wheeler. Molly stood and watched until they disappeared over the rise behind the farm house on the way up to Meg's place. There had been maybe four inches of new snow overnight and the sky still looked ominous, but the landscape was soft and lovely. They went back into the kitchen for coffee and began their meeting. Harry couldn't be reached by phone until later.

"You get your portrait shot, Mike"

"You can look at some of the digital stuff any time you want, but the film is out for a couple days. I found a pretty good lab in town here, but they are a little slow. Proofs day after tomorrow. Harry is anxious for a peek, too. How's your gig going?"

Molly always needed to move when she was thinking. She went to the fridge and got a bottle of water, an apple, and a pear out and placed them on the table before an amused Mike.

"Are you hungry or doing a still life," Mike quipped.

Molly looked at the food. "Oh yeah, if I could paint. My job, as you know is to write and frankly this job has me a bit flustered."

"How so?"

"Well, ponder this, Mike. So far all I have in the way of bio is so typical that it borders on the mundane. Local small town boy sows a few wild oats, does a tour in Nam and comes back fucked up. Nothing new there. He marries his hometown sweetheart, instead of her sister, and because of the war drinks himself into a divorce. He pisses off everyone he knows and becomes a barfly. He writes a few bad books, but somehow gets one or two published because they are war stories. Bargain table stuff. But, then somewhere along the line he becomes one of the most revered writers in America. The world, for God's sake. How the heck did that happen?"

"Have you asked him?"

"No, not yet, but everyone else is telling me to do that very thing. Only I don't know how to lead him to it yet. The man is so darn nice I am having a hard time asking him about how he went from prickhood to sainthood."

"Hah, you'll get it. We've only been here a few days," Mike said while yawning.

"And that's the other thing that bothers me."

"What?"

"Don't you feel like you have been here longer? Like years? Actually, I even feel like I have been here before."

"Déjà vu?"

"Stronger than that. Do you feel anything like that, Mike?"

Mike played with the stem of the pear, thinking. "Okay, now that you mention it, I do have some strange feeling about this place. Not just the house, but Pipe."

"Oh yeah?"

"I travel a lot right? I've been everywhere, but there is something about this little town. I don't feel like an outsider. I have a strong sense of connection here."

"You may be having a strong reaction to that bartender. What's her name, Carrie?"

"Yeah, Carrie. Maybe, but it is more than that. It is a connection to you, Roland, and the kids. This farm. Kind of a family thing. It's like I can't wait to get up in the morning. I never felt that before."

"My thing is something like that, too. Weird, huh? And the girl?"

"We had a sort of fight last night." He grimaced as he said the words.

"Oh, shit, you didn't hit her? I noticed your hand is swollen."

Mike looked at his hand like he had just discovered it was attached to his wrist. "God no! But, I did hit her husband."

In the next ten minutes Mike related the story of Crazy Ray and Carrie and described the infamous punch with a hint of bravado. Molly was pie-eyed listening to the account, believing and yet not believing it. Wiry Mike, the soft-eyed shutter bug in a bar fight with a rock and roll rooster. She almost pulled out the tape recorder.

"So how does it stand with her now?"

"Don't know. First time in my life I was the knight in shining armor and she didn't buy the act. What do you think I should do?"

Molly bit the apple while she decided how this story should progress. "Go back down there. That's really what you both want."

"I don't know."

"I do! And here's another tip. Ask her out, you dope. Meeting her at the place where she is working every night is way bush league. Court her up proper there, Jethro. Are all you guys that dense?"

"Don't lump me in with all those guys, Molly. I know a couple guys you dated and they gave assholes a bad name."

"Really! Like who?"

"Like that congressman. Shit, a Republican, Molly! How could you? And then there was that relief pitcher for the Sox."

"He was an asshole. Okay, both of them, but you don't have to be like them. That's my point, Mikey. Do something unexpected. Break the mold. Change."

"Like Roland did."

Mike's simple observation shut down Molly's rant. She was looking at Mike, but saw someone else. In her mind she saw Roland when he was young, messed up, and careless. Then she saw Roland as he was today, kind, soulful, and talented. Where in heaven or on earth was the door where men could pass through and change. She knew she needed to work on the answer. It was the whole key to her story. The first part of Roland's life was worthless except for the fact that it led him to the second part. She bit the apple again, a Midwestern Eve in the Garden of Wisconsin.

Mike waited in the van across the street from The Back Room as the last of the regulars filed out and headed back to their farms and beds. He had sketched out a plan on how to approach Carrie all day and this was the best he could do; wait outside in the cold. Within minutes the lights began to go off inside and when the bar finally went dark he found himself staring at the door and holding his breath. He got out of the van and leaned against the door. In what seemed like an eternity, Carrie finally emerged into the pale light of the Heineken sign, put her head down, and crossed the street toward him.

"Carrie." he said when she got to the middle of Highway 151. She stopped in her tracks.

"Mike?"

"Yeah. Can we talk for a minute?"

Carrie remained motionless in the road. She looked north and south, but there was nothing moving that time of night. "Might take more than a minute."

"I've got all night." He felt some relief beginning to seep into him. She finally walked across the final lane and stood in front of him. He could just make out her face from a little light in the window of the meat market. He thought she looked beautiful, her blonde hair slightly moving in the night breeze.

"I'm hungry. You?" she said, but still was not smiling.

"Maybe. Where do we go this time of night?"

"Gotta go into Fondy. There's a twenty-four hour coffee shop on Main."

"Let's go. The van is all warmed up."

Driving into town, the front seats of the van seemed to be miles apart. There was not much conversation, but once inside the Four Doves Restaurant, under bright lights with the delicious smell of coffee and bacon in the air, their muteness ended. She talked, he listened.

"Live music is big here in Wisconsin. You know, the bar scene and all that. A lot of us were groupies back then here in Fond du Lac and Ray was a local star and everyone knew he would make it someday. Well, okay, one day he made it with me and the next day he made it in the biz. He got a record deal and I got a baby. I actually, thought I loved him for a while. My folks made sure he married me so the kid would not be a bastard. That's funny looking back because big bastards make little bastards. My son must have inherited every possible bad gene from his dad because he made my life miserable, too. I was not all that upset when he ran off and joined his dad.

"I'm not telling you this for sympathy, Mike. I was terrible back then, too. I guess you could say I was a bad mother since my mom raised and spent more time with Ray Jr. than I did. I was always working in bars and then hanging out in them. At least Crazy Ray made a name for himself and lots of money. I was just a joke. You know, Mrs. Crazy Ray. Neither one of us acted like we were married. Ever. Ray sent me some money, but it was inconsistent and I never did anything for the kid with it. I spent it all on myself.

"One day I just got tired of that scene and the endless bar time guys taking me home. I moved out to Pipe and got my place above the butcher. The Back Room is populated by old geezers mostly who don't bother me. Guys who put their teeth in a glass next to their beer. Before guys used to hit on me because I was Crazy Ray's wife. I knew that and let them. You could say I had a little self-esteem problem. My customers now never heard of Ray...until you decked him, that is. I'm telling you all this because of what you did last night. I acted mad because I didn't know what else to do. No one, and I mean no one ever stood up for me. That you did it with him was amazing, but it scared me, too. I get confused pretty easy. I'm confused right now."

The plates of breakfast food arrived just then, blueberry waffles and sausages. Neither Mike nor Carrie even looked at the plates. They just stared at each other. Carrie waited for a verdict on her history lecture and semi-apology and Mike waited for the careful words he would eventually speak.

"So all this happened and then we fast forward to the other night when we met. We have both had other lives. I am not sure I could even begin to tell you about mine. My behavior has not always been a model for anyone. But, you know, when I hit Ray I might have just turned some sort of corner. I hit him for you, Carrie. Because nobody calls someone I love that word."

Carrie was quickly replaying the last sentence. There was a misplaced word in there.

"You love me?"

"I don't know. It feels like it."

"How does it feel?"

"It feels like those are the best blueberry waffles I have ever seen and I can't even lift a fork. I can't eat, I can't sleep, I can barely work, and I'm feeling like Pipe, Wisconsin is the center of the universe. And all I can think about is you. It's like everything else I ever felt before was just a crush. Like I just got to the big leagues. Like its Spring instead of Winter. Should I go on?"

Carrie simply shook her head. She pushed her plate aside and called the waitress over and asked for the check.

"Let's go home. I want you to read to me and rub my back."

At certain times in your life you just know. You stop acting and leave the theater. You go home and begin the next phase of your life. Sometimes all the rage and guilt, shame and bitterness are left on the table with the tip and you just go home. You just know something bad is over and something good has begun.

CHAPTER FOURTEEN

You have experienced the dream within the dream. You think you wake up from one and realize on some level that you have entered another. Garnet Granger had perfected the art of dreaming in multiple layers. She dove so far into her slumber that the dream depth became infinite. If she began to wake from one she would, by force of will, build up a cushion of a dozen more. Dreams of flying would never let her land. Dreams of ocean bottoms never required breath. Dreams of love were never unrequited. Dreams of dreams were never disturbed. The Waking World was just a distant star whose light had first burst out a million light years ago and, now long dead, still emitted a ghost light into the cosmos. It was there but not there, like the dreamer. She had perfected the art of becoming a single photon in the spectrum of a million, million dreams and she had entered a worm hole, the tap root of time in the seam of all dimensions, speeding away faster than light into the center of everywhere. She heard her mother's faint voice calling for her to awaken, but she tuned out its urgent sweetness and reached out for a boney hand. And everywhere there were birds.

Thursday morning came up clear and white as if all the world had been purified during the night. Roland was the first one stirring, throwing off his Hudson Bay blanket and finding himself surprised and stiff having spent the night in a chair. The former cheese shed, now studio was already collecting light although the sun would not crest The Ledge for another forty minutes. His first thought was that he wished the dog was still around so they could walk. His second thought was that he would be seeing the dog soon enough. He had another date at the clinic today. Roland knew that his very honest Chinese oncologist would tell him in a couple hours that yesterday's tests did not look good. It did not bother him because sometimes an hour could be a day and a day could be a lifetime. He pondered that men who have made their peace awake this way and then go easy into the day.

Roland tinkered with the wood stove and found just enough ember remaining to begin a new fire. Once that was done he went outside to relieve himself and startled some sparrows and nuthatches that were hanging around his door working the beaten snow for food. He usually threw a little suet out for the birds when the weather was brutal, though he knew they could feed themselves just fine. But, then he liked to have them come into the yard so he could watch them. He admired their wings.

When he was done with Dr. Lu he would pay a visit to his lawyer. There was a laundry list of legal loose ends that needed to be braided. It was getting harder and harder to get the energy up to leave Ghost Farm and run errands in town. He saw a light come on in the kitchen and then managed to catch a glimpse of Molly go by the window. He knew she was making coffee. Rather than hurry into the house, he watched the window for a moment. Molly was framed by light as she worked at the sink. Her hair was messy and she was in a robe. He noticed immediately that it was his old blue terry cloth robe that hung on a hook behind the bed room door. He liked that she was wearing it, but wasn't exactly sure why. He went in the kitchen door and the first shaft of winter sunlight lit it as he closed it behind him.

"Good morning, Roland," Molly croaked hoarsely. She was barely awake. "I wanted to get the coffee made and do the dishes before the girls wake up and start dirtying them again."

Roland sat down at the table and smiled at his guest. "You look like you're sleepwalking, Molly. Better make that coffee strong."

Molly finished pouring the water into the automatic coffee maker and switched it on. "I had a strange night. The girls slept in Mike's room, but I still couldn't sleep very well. I had these strange dreams all night."

"That bed is a good dreaming bed, I've found. You remember any of them?"

Molly sat down across from Roland. "I kept dreaming about the lake. Your lake. The big one out there."

"Winnebago."

"Yeah. I was out there walking around all the little houses, knocking on doors, and no one would let me in. I woke up and I was inside one of the houses and it was this house, but I was still asleep. And then the ice began to crack below me. That time I really did wake up, but I was in your bed so again I didn't know where I was at first. Weird huh?"

Roland leaned back in his chair and crossed his legs. He had slept in his clothes so he realized he was wrinkled and his hair was mussed up. He ran his hands through his hair with little effect. "Sometimes dreams represent a latent desire. I think you want or need to go out on the lake. You have been looking out on it for several days, but we have never discussed it."

"I suppose."

"I think we need to do it," said Roland, tapping his finger on the table.

"Do what?"

"This afternoon's interview will take place in a fish shanty. One of the little houses on Winnebago. You can answer the call of your dream while you do you job. Multi-tasking."

"The girls will want to go, too. You realize that right?"

Roland nodded and then spoke. "You and me in one ice house and the girls and Mike in another."

"I'm not sure he would do it."

"Last time I checked he was working for your magazine taking pictures. It would be a great photo op since he has shot the heck out of me and everything else around the farm."

"I suppose."

"Where did you pick up that 'I suppose' thing? That is so local."

"I suppose." Molly was now smiling and went to get the coffee. As she poured she knew the story of Roland's wife would be told in a fish shanty on Lake Winnebago. She liked the angle. Angle?

"Are we going to fish or just talk?" She set the cups on the table.

"I can get some gear. We'll do both, okay?"

"The girls will love it."

"Good. I'll make the arrangements when I am out this morning. A little change of scenery is always good."

"You said last night you had to go to the doctor again this morning."

"Doctor and lawyer. Keeps the economy moving. I am getting some test results is all"

Molly noticed Roland was suddenly not smiling and she regretted having mentioned the doctor visit. It was too early to be tactful. "I'm sorry I mentioned your appointment, Roland."

He took a sip of hot joe and winced. "Why be sorry, dear. We are just family sitting at the kitchen table, having morning coffee, and discussing the affairs of the day." He set down the cup and looked at Molly, waiting until her eyes came up to meet his. "It's a good word, right, Molly?"

"What?"

"Family."

She looked into those gray eyes and saw the winter light. She smiled and stood up and walked around to his side of the table. From behind his chair she put her arms around his neck and, while hugging him, laid her head against his head. Families did this sort of thing, she thought. She gave him a peck on the top of his head and then went around and took her cup in hand.

"I want to be first in the shower. I need the hot water."

"What are you going to do this morning while I am gone?"

"Write."

Roland smiled and nodded. She had said the magic word.

Mike Gabler and Carrie Stirling were watching the prisms, cast by a dangling crystal, dance on the wall of her bedroom above the Pipe Meat Market. The light was almost as magical as the night had been. They had finished *The Tap Root* together with Mike reading as promised. The back rub has quickly turned into lovemaking before they could discuss the ending. Now Carrie was propped up and re-reading the ending. Mike thought she was especially sexy with her glasses on. The reading glasses made her blue eyes even bigger; blue camera lens aimed at him.

"I want to meet him," said Carrie, while looking at Roland's picture on the back cover.

"I think he would like that," said Mike, turning on his elbow to face her.

"Why?"

"I told him about you."

"Oh god, I can imagine what you told him."

"You should imagine it. I told him I got struck by lightning down the road."

"That's cute," she said. Then thinking it over, "That's nice."

"Tomorrow is Friday. He said it is a local tradition to go out for fish on Friday."

"That's an understatement."

"He told me to invite you to go out with us. So you see, he wants to meet you, too."

Carrie looked at Mike and blinked the huge eyes. She smiled with just the tip of her tongue sticking through her perfect teeth. "You think he would autograph this book for my mom?"

"I think he would do anything for you if you smile at him like that."

"Do you have the day off?" She had changed the subject very subtly and Mike noticed.

"Yeah, maybe. Roland is not going to be around this morning. Why?"

"Well, it just so happens I have the day off, too. I have an appointment in town at 9 AM and I was wondering if you would go with me."

Mike sensed something in her voice that told him to proceed with caution. "What's up?"

"I am going to court today." She waited for a response that only came from Mike's questioning eyes and eyebrows. "The divorce is being heard today."

Mike now raised his head up and put a pillow behind it. This sort of thing required the head to be raised. At least it clarified whether Ray was and ex or not. He obviously wasn't quite. "You want me to go to court with you? I am not sure that would be a good idea, Carrie. Don't you think Ray might start something with me again? Maybe ruin your court date?"

"Well, first of all, he probably won't show up. He doesn't have to. Secondly, I talked to him last night and he is not mad at you. He wanted me to tell you that."

"What did he say?"

"He said he if he had known we were seeing each other he would never have made that comment. He didn't know we even knew each other. When he figured it all out, he said you did the right thing and..." Carrie was looking for proper phrasing. "And that little shit gets punched out a couple times a month. It's not that big a deal And...."

"And?"

"And he said he wished us well."

Mike pondered this for a second. The word 'us' was what Carrie had stumbled over. Mike knew all the subtext evoked by using that word. It was a kind of pre-marriage in itself. He knew you either corrected it now or it began a contract that meant much more than the sum of its two letters. He looked at the bespectacled woman next to him and noticed a prism had fallen on her left breast, the one that covered her heart. He wasn't looking for a sign because his mind was already made up, but it was a nice touch, he thought.

"I wish us well, too."

The glasses came off, the book was set aside and Mike and Carrie did a radical change of position in the bed. Very soon the prism of rainbow light was swaying on Mike's upper back.

"We're going fishing today." Melanie was at one end of the ancient bathtub and her little sister was at the other. Bubble bath made them look like they were chest deep in clouds.

"How are we going to fish? It is too cold, Mel. The water is hard," observed little Sonia with African logic.

"Mom says we go into one of those little houses on the big lake and fish through a hole in the ice. Neat, huh?"

"And the ice will hold us?" The mystery of ice and snow was still something the Sub-Saharan mind at any age could only grasp with doubts.

"Mom says it is three feet thick. Cars and trucks can drive out on it."

"I guess it is okay, then, huh Mel?"

"Yeah, and Mike is going with us."

Sonia did not quite share her sister's crush on Mike, but she did know she loved everything about him. The mere mention of Mike's name made Sonia's big brown eyes widen and smile. "Mike is coming to fish with us?"

Melanie smiled and nodded.

"You love Mike, Melanie." There was a childish, little sister taunt in Sonia's decree.

"You don't even know what that means, Sony."

"You love Mike!" Sonia whipped the top off a soap cloud in her sister's direction. Melanie responded in kind. The shrieks and giggling drew Molly into the bathroom.

"You girls get out of there and get dressed. We are going sightseeing with Mrs. Bollander this morning."

"Melanie loves Mike!" Sonia would not set a working needle aside.

"She can love who she wants. Now get out of there."

The girls climbed out of the tub and toweled themselves off. It was cold upstairs and they found themselves shivering and hurrying to get dry. In the big bed room, their suitcases were still open on the floor and Molly rummaged for clean clothes for them.

"We are going to have to do wash today, too," Molly noted.

"Mom, is Mike coming with us today?" Melanie asked in a whisper.

"No not this morning, he is with his friend again. But, he is going fishing with us later." Molly immediately saw the question marks in Melanie's eyes. "Mel, Mike has found a friend here and he is spending some time with...her." She, of course, knew about her daughter's crush and had avoided discussing it. Now it was on the table.

"It's a girl?" said Melanie. Three words full of wonder, hurt, and betrayal.

"Yes, Mel, a very nice woman named Carrie. I know you like Mike, but he is a grown man and you are a girl. Anyway, you are going to meet Carrie tomorrow tonight for supper, I think. I also think you are going to like her."

Melanie wasn't buying any of this news. "I don't want to meet her. And I don't care about Mike." She pouted as he got dressed. Fortunately, Sonia had gone back into the bathroom to brush her hair.

Molly knew this was one of those predictable scenarios of growing up. She had been there, but now she was supposed to be the wise, old mother. Dealing with her daughters and the men in their lives was going to be tricky. It was not her strong suit, she reminded herself. In fact it was her weakest suit. She had stood in the open field of relationships many times waiting for the lightning to strike her. It just never had. In order to break the tension, she turned on an ancient bed-side radio; the kind with the wooden frame and sweeping hand dial. Surprisingly, it worked, spewing loud polka music into the room. More surprisingly, it worked some sort of magic.

"What is that music?" Melanie asked, her face looking like she had just eaten a sour grape.

"Polka music. Don't you like it?"

"Yuck!"

Molly took Melanie's hands and began to dance her around the room. Neither one of them knew exactly what they were doing, but soon they were both laughing. Sonia raced in from the bathroom to see what was going on and joined them immediately. Frankie Yankovich rolled over in his grave somewhere and beamed.

CHAPTER FIFTEEN

I have heard of love spoken of in terms of chemistry, but it may more accurately be described in the darker language of alchemy. People pass, meet, bump into each other daily and yet the spark of connection rarely flares up, despite the presence of fuel (sensuality), oxygen (mating urges), and ignition (lust). My observation is that more movement is begun by the elemental combining of earth (location), wind (chance), and water (mystery). The odds of meeting the love of your life within the span of your years are infinitesimal. And I mean true love, not this dart-thrown gamble that we are more than ready to dive into. Having said all of this, I believe I was kissed by fate when I met the woman who was to be my wife. I could literally feel the ions surrounding the nuclei of every atom in my being start to reverse their field and direction. I felt zero gravity in her presence. I touched the sun on her mouth. Alas, it was half a miracle, which is to say it was none at all. Like an alchemist, I drew the solid gold of her heart away and sold it for a sad song. My miracle was her curse, and thus mine, too. It was the only thing we shared beyond our vows. And it was too long a road on down to ruin to have been merciful.

The Law Firm of Zaneb, Charon, and Marek always sounded to Roland more like the stars in Orion's belt than a group of small town lawyers. Their office on Main Street near the county court house in Fond du Lac was a refurbished Amish furniture store that had long ago gone out of business. Roland always wondered, but never asked if the old store's wares were delivered by horse and wagon to its customers. The irony that the holy folks had been replaced by the devil's advocates was not invisible to him.

Patrick Zaneb was an old childhood friend of Roland's; a rare friend who had stuck with him through the thickness and thinness of his life. Outside of the divorce initiated by Karin, they had rather limited professional contact over the years. In the past month they had seen each other more than in the past fifty years. Roland now had preparations to make and little time to enact them. Patrick was looking at a dwindling amount of billable hours, but he was also looking at an old friend, who needed his help.

"Rollie, for God's sake, I can do some of this stuff in the time frame you have given me, but for the love of God, this other thing is not budging."

Roland knew Pat to be a godless man and the fact that he evoked the Almighty multiple times in sentences endeared the man to him. "The last thing is just as important as the first thing. What's the problem, anyway? I am offering a huge amount of money for this accommodation. What's the snag?"

They were seated at Patrick's desk, an Amish antique holdover, and the sun, coming in over the buildings across the street, was blinding Roland as he spoke. There were no shades on the windows, which was part of the stark design that Pat favored. His partners had lush offices of leather and thick carpet, but Pat liked to use his office as a subtle display of his honesty and frugality. He was, indeed, beloved for these craftily tailored traits.

"The money is right, Rollie, it's the damned red tape, for the love of God. We've got some time right? I'll keep making the calls. I'll call the goddamned governor if I have to.

"What's wrong?" Pat was reading his friends face. He saw something there he didn't like.

"Just came from the doc, Patrick. I may not make it to the lilacs this Spring and I need these details tied up. Now, I paid you a big advance to get this stuff rolling, but you won't get a dime from the estate unless our business is completed. And don't look at me like that. You don't look so good yourself, counselor."

Pat Zaneb sighed deeply and made a tent of his fingers on the desk. "God help me, Rollie. I'll get this done for you, but there are one or two things you are going to have to explain to me."

"Like?"

"Like why in the name of God are you doing this? It seems like a complete waste of money. Isn't there better, hell, more sane things you could be doing with your estate? You're spending a fortune on what, a whim?"

"You've known me forever, Pat. Would I do something crazy?" Roland knew this was the tension breaker. Most of his dealings with Pat, early and late in life, had a touch of crazy in them.

"You would and have. Where you off to now?" Pat asked almost as an afterthought.

"Going ice fishing."

"You're goddamn kidding, right?"

"Nope."

"Shit! Get the hell out of here. I have work to do, goddamn it," swore Patrick and he punctuated it with a fist to the desk. Roland stood and they shook hands, both trying hard not to break down laughing...or crying.

On his way home Roland drove down to Manawa Beach and banged on the door of a small cottage that had every sort of lawn ornament known to man parked in its yard. Snow White and the Seven Dwarves looked a little cold in the snow, but the small herd of deer looked as comfortable as the gazing balls and miniature light houses. A rather large woman came to the door looking angry, but she melted into a smile when she saw Roland.

"Well, look who come knockin' at my door. Get in here, Roland."

Barbara Dorfman was a second cousin of Roland's and her husband, Mort was a dear old friend. Roland was feeling a little guilty to come calling since he rarely was down this way anymore. When Barb got him inside and she yelled for Mort to come see who was there. Roland heard a toilet flush and then Mort appeared with his hand out and a big grin on his face.

"Well Roland, you old shit. What bring you down off The Ledge to the lake for cry-eye?" asked Mort as he wrung Roland's hand. Barb stood by beaming. Roland was the only celebrity in the family and any visit was royally welcomed.

"I came down to see if you could help me set up a little ice fishing party for this afternoon."

"What do ya need, Rollie?" Mort led Roland to a slightly worn easy chair and pushed him down. Barb went to get coffee.

"I need a couple houses and the usual rigs. Bait, too, of course. Anything biting these days?"

"Mostly perch, couple walleye. My shed is out yonder there and I think I can get the neighbors for a couple bucks. Gear ain't no problem. Who ya fishin' with?"

"Got some folks in from Boston doing a little article on me and I though I'd show them a little local sport fishing."

Barbara came into the living room with the coffee. Roland noticed it was the good china. He was humbled by the gesture. These were simple folks in their seventies now, he reckoned. Real nice people and again he felt guilty for living so close to family and not seeing them more often.

"Well, Mort will fix you up, won't you, honey? You like it black as I recall, Rollie."

"Yes, thanks, Barbie." It was getting cozy already. Old family could close a gap pretty quickly.

"We read about the latest prize. We are so proud of you, Roland," Barb added. "'Course we're no readers so we don't know your books, but they must be wonderful."

This kind of admission always stumped Roland. How could people just declare themselves non-readers and beg off like it was something like playing golf. Hell, maybe in their minds it was, he thought. It didn't matter. He was using them for their fishing equipment and placement on the lake. And he hated fishing.

After another ten minutes of 'have-you-seen-so-and-so' small talk, Roland excused himself, promising to be back down in a couple hours. The Dorfman's were delighted and walked him out to his truck, prompting more handshakes and kisses. That chore checked off, he headed back to the highway and home. Sonia was waiting for him at the door.

"Papa, Papa, are we really going fishing on the icy lake?"

Roland scooped her up in his arms, not even thinking in that moment that he was a sick man. "Yes, little one, we are going fishing on the icy lake!" Sonia buried her face in his coat collar and squeezed him. At that moment Mike's van pulled up to the house and Sonia was quickly trying to get down to greet him, too. Roland caught Molly's eye just inside the door.

"Where's Melanie?" he asked her.

"Sulking upstairs," said Molly.

Roland was quick on this one uptake. "She found out about Mike's girl at the bar?"

Molly nodded with a strange knowing smile. "Think we should be shutting them up together in an ice shanty, Roland?"

"It might be just the thing."

"We're gonna find out, I guess."

"Oh Molly, I am sorry if my idea of everyone being here is causing problems." He said it in a way that she knew he didn't mean it. Molly knew Roland was loving the company and the mini-soap opera.

"It'll be a nice warm up for your fish fry party tomorrow. Might be some real fireworks when the two ladies finally meet," said Molly and then once again, driven by pure instinct, she gave Roland a big hug. He hugged her back hard, happy to be welcomed into this own house.

Carrie's long overdue divorce had gone anti-climactically smooth earlier in the day. Mike had sat with her nervously while her lawyer, Anne Bedoes-Pankratz read the petition. Since Crazy Ray had traveled all the way back to Wisconsin for the event, they had expected him to show up, but he didn't, much to Mike's relief. The divorce was granted and that was that. However, when Mike and Carrie were walking down the courthouse steps, they saw the white stretch limo parked in the loading zone. Apparently there was going to be a parting shot from the rock star. Carrie didn't flinch or miss a step, but walked right up to the car. Mike stayed two steps behind as the tinted glass window was lowered and Ray's smiling face appeared.

"Is everybody happy now?" he crooned. Apparently, he was. Carrie noticed there were two young girls in the limo behind Ray and one of them she thought she recognized from the bar.

"Yeah, I'm happy," Carrie said cheerfully. "We should have done this years ago."

"We should have never been married years ago, Carrie.

"No shit."

"I'll tell Ray Jr. you said hello."

"Don't bother."

"Bitch!"

"Asshole!"

The tinted window went up as if some final initial had been inked onto the divorce papers. The limo lurched into the street and Carrie, who had never changed her name anyway, went back to being legally single. She noted that very little had changed until she turned around and looked at Mike. He had a little camera up to his face and he took her picture in that first instant of freedom.

"What's that for?" she asked, not angry, but a little off guard.

"I have no idea," Mike said. He did, but didn't admit it. It was his first picture of her as his. They decided to celebrate later as Mike had an ice fishing date to get to.

There girls were excited when Mort Dorfman drove them out to the ice shanties on his old snowmobile. It was still a spectacularly clear day and the sun reflected brightly off the green and gold, respectively, ice houses owned by Mort and his neighbor. Mort spent a little more time with Mike, Melanie, and Sonia than he did with Roland and Molly because Roland had told him there wasn't going to be much fishing going on in their shanty. He got the hole open for the girls and showed them and Mike how to set the trip lines. He had put them in his shiny gold shanty because he knew the neighbor's Packer green house was decorated with girlie pictures and had a liquor locker. He knew because that's where he spent most of his own fishing time. His own shanty was mostly for Barb when she and her girlfriends wanted to go out on the ice to bitch about men and try their luck.

As soon as everyone was settled Mort drove back across the quarter mile of ice to his house with a promise to check back in an hour or so. Melanie has been predictably sullen with Mike, but she was too young a woman to stay at war for long. Molly left them all giggling as she walked back to the gold shanty and her interview with Roland. Before she entered, she took a long look around her. The white expanse of Lake Winnebago was awesome, only broken by the myriad of ice houses and the occasional roar of a snowmobile. She was struck by how alien this place was and yet, how perfectly beautiful. Her eyes scanned back to the east and found Roland's yellow barn on The Ledge. It looked as gold as Mort's shanty in the afternoon sun. She sighed, smiled to herself, and went inside.

"I caught a perch already," Roland announced, while holding up a stiff little fish.

"Wow! I hope they have some luck over there or the girls are going to get bored quickly. I think they liked the speed of the snowmobile more than they will the fishing."

"They both like being with Mike so they won't be bored," Roland observed. "Besides, he's said he brought cameras for both of them. Got a feeling we are going to have a very long slide show after dinner."

"I bet you're right." With that, Molly fished out her tape recorder and set it on a little folding canvas stool. It was a not too subtle hint that there was work to do. Roland looked at the device and aimed his predictable frown in its direction. "You ready?" she asked.

"I suppose. I don't want to have to repeat any of this because it hurts me to talk about her. I am gonna trust you to be discreet when you write or refer to this part of my story, okay?"

"Roland, don't you trust me yet? This part...today is for my background. There are some things I need to know. Something I am looking for. I would never write anything to embarrass you."

Roland nodded and took his fishing line out of the water. He looked around the small shed and glanced at the girlie pictures. While they were relatively tame pictures, they did provide a silent, unwanted audience for his story. He remembered the confessional booths of his Catholic youth and this place was so very different and yet the effect was similar. Molly switched on the recorder and this was the voice of the ice fishing afternoon:

Karin Bollander was a girl I had secretly admired for a long time before I even spoke to her. She was about four years younger than me so we needed to grow up a bit to where age gaps were closed. We didn't have much contact in school, but I would see her at church and around town at fairs and picnics, you know. Anyway, sometimes there is a person that you just can't take your eyes off of for what ever reason. Not sure what that little thing is that causes that. Anyway, I liked her for a long time, secretly. Never told a soul how I felt.

Somewhere in there I began to notice her sister, Meg. She was only a couple years younger than me and that put us together more. I couldn't help, but notice that she liked me and it was one of those things where I was looking over my shoulder at Karin and Meg stepped into view, blocking out her sister for a while. I don't think I was ever conscious that I was using Meg to get close to Karin, but who knows what's going on in kid's heads when they're starting to pair up for life? So, Molly, I guess I went too far with Meg. She was a willing conquest and it was a big deal back then to go all the way. Big deal for the guy and the girl. It sort of meant more then, I guess; like a promise. I made that promise over and over again to Meg one summer. And then something happened.

As I remember it, we were doubling with Karin and some other guy. Don't even recall his name. I remember feeling relieved that she had a boyfriend. It took my heart off of some sort of hook. If she was unattainable then I was with the next best girl, her sister. Boy, that sounds cheesy now, Molly. Forgive me and all of my gender for that kind of logic.

Anyway, one night we dropped the boyfriend off and were driving home. I remember this part as clear as if it was happening right now. I ended up holding hands with Karin behind Meg's back. Karin had initiated it. I guess she had come to some sort of crossroads all on her own. By that simple act, she had taken me away from Meg and everyone sort of changed partners. Karin and I began a love that ended in marriage. Meg and I began a bitter divide that ended in her hating me for life. If that wasn't enough, what I did later on would destroy all three of us.

We've talked about some of this before. I came back from Viet Nam in '65 and got married in '66. I think I got drunk at my own wedding and never quite sobered up. Yeah, I had issues, but like I said before, I internalized them. Karin had a good job at Mercury and so she had a little life of her own. She was able to tolerate me because she was out of the house, but she also did it to make Meg think we were doing okay. I also believe we thought that some kids would come along and that would change everything. They didn't. It was always deemed to be 'God's will' and I agreed. Why would God send innocent babies to a father like me? Anyway, on New Year's Eve of '81 the whole thing blew up. Mt. Roland finally erupted after spewing smoke and ash for many years. I gotta make this short, Molly because I can hardly bear the memory. As drunk as I was that night, my mind has recorded it vividly and with great detail.

Karin and I got home from a neighbor's party and she went into a fit about my behavior. We had a house in Fond du Lac back then on 5th Street. Anyway, I guess you could say her volcano had reached its blowing point, too. She went around the house and smashed all of the booze bottles in the cabinets. She took all of the beer bottles out of the fridge in the basement and broke them against the walls down there. I remember the walls dripping with foam downstairs and the stink of whiskey upstairs. There was broken glass everywhere. When she was finished breaking bottles she lit into me. Yeah, I remember the words, but I will never repeat them, so just use your imagination. (Sigh) I hauled off and hit her, Molly. I smashed her in the face. There was blood everywhere, but she never went down. She just stared at me with the darkest hatred I had ever seen. I stormed out and woke up in a snow drift a couple hours later, half frozen. I immediately remembered what had happened and went home. The place was empty, but the glass and other mess had been cleaned up, basement, too. What remained was the blood on the carpet and the kitchen floor.

In the morning the police came and told me Karin had been to the emergency room and they wanted to know what I knew about it. I wasn't ready to confess anything and they left. I had figured out that she was not telling them anything or pressing charges or I would have gone to jail. By not owning up to the facts, I sentenced myself to a worse prison. A life sentence for that night.(Sigh) Long story short, okay. This is hard. Meg and Karin would tell you not hard enough. Karin never came home. I got divorce papers in exchange for not having her press charges. I signed them and never showed up in court. I let her go. She moved to California, I heard and the only other contact we had was when I sold the house and gave the entire sum to her lawyer to send to her. I heard through the grapevine over the years that she got remarried and still lives as a widow in a place called Goleta. I looked it up on a map and it is on the ocean, which I hope is a peaceful place. As far as I can tell she doesn't communicate with her sister and I suppose that is my fault, too. I made a mess, Molly, and it is never gonna get cleaned up.

You might think those two Pulitzer books were some sort of atonement? Well, I hope they are for some of my readers. They were merely acts of attrition on my part. I didn't write them for Karin or Meg, for that matter. I wrote them to God. And not for forgiveness. I wrote them to let him know I was still here and that some people could actually break out of Hell if they were willing to uninvent it. That's right, Molly, I see your look. Uninvent Hell. We'll talk about that next time. Right now I really need to get out of this shanty and see what your girls are up to.

At the end of this long day, Molly took careful notice how quiet Roland was the rest of the evening. After supper they all got a game of Monopoly going at the kitchen table and the competitive girls were really going all in for it. Mike stayed until he went bankrupt and then quietly disappeared, presumably to see Carrie again. Roland was doing his best for the girl's sake, but Molly knew he had ripped himself up in the fish shanty. It was hard to watch and even harder to listen when she replayed the tape after the kids went to bed. Roland the sweet old man and Roland the drunken wife-beater didn't settle in her mind no matter how hard she tried to justify it. She played the last part of it over a couple times. "Uninvent Hell." She knew this was what she was looking for. The missing key to not only the two wonderful novels, but to Roland's creative soul. *Art Harvest* was certainly not a psychology journal, but it was about artists and how they ticked. "Listen for the tick," Harry had always told her.

CHAPTER SIXTEEN

I never traveled much in my life. I guess that trip to Southeast Asia ruined my wanderlust forever. Most of the people around here don't travel too much. Oh, they get the yearly trip to Las Vegas on some cheap junket and get their pictures taken in front of Caesar's Palace with a drink in their hand, but not too many folks go abroad. Because of this a sort of xenophobia has set in. Strangers are considered strange. Foreigners are foreign. There is a kind of almost benign racism that grows out of rarely seeing anyone who looks different from you. Ethnic jokes in bars are tolerated because no one is hurt by them. In truth, a Flatlander, a Yooper, or some Ufda Minnesotan is more often the butt of local joke.

White people who follow a sports team from a different state are loathed unashamedly. And the enmity is very real. I remember feeling that way when I was younger. Then one day I made a deal with the devil. Harry Stompe was a hated Chicago Bears fan, but he was also a man with the key to my success. He pointed out to me my state's inherited inferiority complex. I thanked him for his help and advice, but always secretly wished that one day he and his damned Bears would enjoy watching the Packers play in the Super Bowl from one of the lowest circles of The Inferno

Yelanek's Supper Club in Jericho was an old and revered Holyland landmark. They knew their customers well and provided the big portions of food and strong drinks that brought many generations of hungry and thirsty folks through their doors. Never was this more true than on Friday nights. The tradition of the Friday night fish fry may have been Catholic in origin, but those darn Lutherans and pesky Methodists knew a good thing when they saw it, too. The place was practically printing money. Food was probably a break even deal, but the bar was the cash cow and getting anywhere near it on Friday night was tough. The Roland Heinz party of six was finding that out, although Mike and Carrie had not joined them yet.

Yelanek's never took reservations. The deal was you gave your name to the hostess and then ordered while you waited at the bar. This technique ensured a big bar tab before dinner was even ordered. The longer the wait, the bigger the bar tab. Roland was watching the bar for any opening that would allow Mel and Sonia a chance to get a bar stool so they could have a Shirley Temple. He also noted that the girls were getting a lot of stares from the other patrons. It was normal, he figured. Melanie's shiny black hair and slim Asian beauty was hard to ignore. Little Sonia, with her huge brown eyes and light brown curls was a beauty in her own right. Roland expelled from his mind any idea that the girls were being stared at because they were the only non-whites in the crowed restaurant, even if there might be a filament of truth in the assumption.

Finally, a group of four left the bar for their tables and Roland pounced on the vacant, yet still warm seats. The girls got seated and their kiddie drinks were ordered. Molly wanted an Old Fashion and so did Roland. When the drinks came they all made a toast and then began to study the menus.

"Roland, there is something I have been wanting to ask you, but I wasn't sure I could," said Molly.

"But, you think now is the time. Go ahead. We certainly have no secrets after this afternoon."

"Well, how come if you used to have such a bad drinking problem that you, well, continue to drink? I mean you told me about that blackout." She was whispering the request in his ear so the girls couldn't hear, but the din of the bar made every conversation intimate.

"Good question. If you notice, I only drink one drink now. I consider it a social grace. I realize that does not square with what you know about alcoholism, right?"

"Well, yeah. I mean my dad drank like codfish. One drink meant ten."

"Me, too...at one time. I simply changed my behavior. I read the rule book and threw it out. I don't wish to be intoxicated, but I do wish to have a drink with friends."

"I'm still not sure I get it."

"It's not voodoo, Molly. It's called changing one's spots. Didn't they always tell you a leopard doesn't change its spots?"

Molly could only nod. Fascinating stuff.

"Meet the changed leopard. I exist!"

"Does this have something to do with your other change? You know, what we are going to talk about tomorrow?"

"Only everything."

At that moment Roland spotted Mike and Carrie making their way through the mob. He waved them over as the girls swiveled on their stools to finally get a look at Mike's girlfriend. Neither Melanie nor Sonia could take their eyes off of Carrie and they were speechless through the first introductions. She looked like a fairy princess to them, wearing a white peasant skirt and white top with silver jewelry. Carrie's hair featured a beaded braid on one side and her makeup was perfect. Molly was equally impressed and Roland was all smiles.

"So good to meet you, Carrie," he began. "Mike has told us so little about you." Carrie got the joke and instantly loved Roland.

"I have been wanting to meet you, too Mr. Heinz"

"Roland," he corrected.

"Yes, Roland. Mike and I just finished *The Tap Root* and loved it."

"I heard you were reading it, dear, so I brought you a copy of A *Winter Light*. It's in the car. Give it to you after supper."

"Wow.Thank you so much," blushed Carrie.

"And you know, Molly, my boss," Mike said turning to Molly.

"Hi again," the two women said simultaneously and they both laughed.

"We sort of met at the bar," Carrie added.

"And Carrie, this is Melanie and Sonia, Molly's girls."

Carrie had been coached by Mike to be careful with Melanie, but his cues weren't necessary. As if by magic, Carrie had instantly become Melanie's idol and Mike was forgotten.

"I love your hair," said Mel. "How did you do that braid thing?"

"I can show you later, okay? Hi, Sonia. What's up?"

"You're pretty."

"Well, thank you, so are you. You both are gorgeous. What do you have there, a Shirley Temple?"

"Yeah," said Sonia.

When Carrie ordered a Shirley Temple for herself she made two friends for life. She scooted in between them and helped them make their menu order when the waitress finally showed up. A half hour later they were seated, with Carrie between Mel and Sonia. Mike didn't mind at all. In fact, he loved seeing Carrie work her charm. He realized that he was proud of her and that was a fabulous feeling to have.

Roland was beaming and nodding to some old acquaintances around the room. He hadn't been out on a Friday for a long time and realized he had been missing something. Since everyone else was occupied, Molly put a soft elbow in Mike's arm. She leaned into him.

"I hate to mix business with pleasure, but I need to know if you think you've got your shots. If you do, you can go back any time you want." She then looked over at Carrie. "How are you going to leave her? Something real happened here, didn't it?"

"I haven't even thought about leaving. Molly, but I have another shoot next week."

"Looks like you two are going to have a serious talk pretty soon."

"No shit."

At that moment big plates of fish, fries, and cole slaw were delivered to the table. There was a lazy susan in the middle of the table laden with olives, pickles, cheese, and rye bread. The Roland Heinz party of six settled into their meal like one big happy family, lost in the background noise of cutlery, laughter, and chewing.

A few miles away, Meg Bollander sat in her living room trying to figure out a way to fill the last couple of hours on a

Friday night so she could go to bed without waking up in the middle of the night. She knew that everyone in the county was out tonight having fun and it was her own fault she was home alone. The fact was, she had hoped Molly would call and invite her out. She would have asked her herself, but she did not want to intrude on what she figured was Roland's party.

Roland. He was never far from her thoughts. In a moment of quiet desperation, Meg decided to take a ride around her property before bed. It was not too cold tonight and it was once again clear and starry. She often did this little survey at night in all seasons. She headed to the barn where the ATV was parked and fired it up. Some pigeons that wintered in the barn were startled and she could hear their flutter, but couldn't see them. In low gear, she headed out on her usual clockwise circle. Across the lake the lights of Oshkosh twinkled in the distance, dancing like low stars on the lake's horizon. The moon was hanging low in the southwest and had a slight orange cast to it. The air was dead calm, which became even more apparent when she drove up beneath the huge wind turbine that was just inside Roland's property.

She knew from studying the articles about them that they self-activated at a wind speed of eight miles per hour. With no wind the blades were motionless. She found the useless beast to be even worse than when it was actually doing something. No wind, no electricity for the lights of Oshkosh. A terrible waste of ugliness. She was about to turn for home when she spotted headlights coming up Roland's drive below her. They're coming back from fish fry, she deduced. Probably Yelanek's. If loneliness could be illustrated it would show a snapshot of Meg sitting beneath the silent turbine and watching Roland and his people come home from Friday night fish fry. Of course, this emptiness was not foreign to Meg. Sadly, she thought, it had become something of an old friend.

Meg waited until she thought they were all in the house so they could not hear her engine start up. Then she aborted the rest of her circumnavigation and headed home by the shortest route. There was a bottle of brandy in her cupboard, some

7-UP, a couple sugar cubes, and a splash of bitters waiting for her and she flew to their promise. Meg did not drink alone often, but this beautiful night had been once again raped by her past and all that was associated with it. It would be a night spent in the chair, the afghan over her, a drink nearby, and sleep no where to be found.

CHAPTER SEVENTEEN

The titles of books and the names of characters have always been something that I agonized over. These births and christenings of the population of my imagination are intricate; sometimes because of their hidden meanings but, more often, for their simplicity. A good book title can be a grabber, but it cannot be chosen solely for its supposed commercial appeal. I have always preferred to find a simple phrase from a line in the book and elevate it to the title. A reader can enjoy an 'ah hah' moment when they discover the title hidden in the weeds of the text. Characters are not that easy. Ethnicity, age, and of course, gender can take you in the right direction of a name, but there is often something else that comes into play. Does the character's name sound like the character? I bow to the subjectivity of this nuance, but I try to work with it, none the less. For instance, my most famous character is named Garnet Granger. On the surface it is a dated and ugly name employing the alliteration of a doting parent. Beneath the surface is a palimpsest of a dark red stone mired in rural mud. The feeling I got after trying this name out was one of heavy, unpolished beauty; doomed to endure ridicule. Perhaps as an athlete, this name might be snappy and strong, but as a hopelessly obese young girl, it is a horrible name. Sorry Garnet, you became who you had to be.

After the fish fry, Mike and Carrie has slipped back into Fond du Lac to catch a movie and then decided to have an Irish coffee at the local Irish Pub. There was a fireplace in the back room away from the noisy bar and the little love seat near the fire was empty and waiting for them. Carrie insisted on getting the drinks. She knew the bartender, who would slip them to her for free if she would return the favor sometime at The Back Room. The Irish Coffee was strong, Mike noted, and the fire was very hot. It was all working to make him a little sleepy after the long day.

"How did you like the film?" he asked Carrie as she settled down next him. She tucked on leg underneath her with her back against the armrest, facing him.

"Well, it was pretty good, but there was no ending. Why do they always do that these days?"

Mike took another sip from his mug. "I don't know. Maybe having no ending is a good thing."

Carrie stared at him. His little turn of phrase had instantly cut to the heart of the matter that she had wanted to discuss. It was exactly why she had chosen this place and quickly he was taking the bait on the first real cast. "Listen Mike, I heard a little of what you and Molly were talking about at dinner."

"You did? It was so noisy in that place I could barely hear her myself."

"I've got bartender's ears. Anyway, when are you leaving?"

Mike reached over and took her hand. "I'll be back, Carrie."

"First things first. When are you leaving?"

"Sunday or Monday, I think. I am doing one more photo session with Roland, but it is outside so the weather will have something to do with it."

"Oh." Mike could see her brain was working hard. Her eyes looked digital.

"I have a shoot back in New England next week. After that I might have some time off."

"Might?" She was aware of her one word responses, but couldn't get any more out.

"You think I am going to disappear, huh?"

"Maybe."

"Like I was never here, right?

This time she could only shrug.

"Fuck this." Mike stood up abruptly letting go of her hand. "Let's go for a walk. It is too damned hot in here to think."

Five minutes later they were walking down Main Street. The Christmas decorations and lights were still strung over the street, out of date now in mid January. They were walking about a foot apart, which didn't suit either one of them, but touching might distract from the business that needed to be transacted. They came to a stop in front of a bookstore. The window display was filled with books that the owner supposed would be on Christmas lists; the popular books by the usual suspect authors.

"No Roland," said Carrie.

"He's probably in the back somewhere."

"If they even have them."

Then a moment happened.

"Carrie, I already told you I love you."

She looked at Mike's reflection in the window. "I know, but it's only been a week. Maybe you don't know what you feel."

"Maybe you don't either."

She started to walk away, but he hooked her arm and stopped her where she was.

"This is insane. We thought that movie was dumb. Look at us. We're playing out our own bad movie like this is the way people are supposed to act. What happened over the past week is not strange or weird, it is fucking wonderful! I would have been gone after the first night if something didn't click inside me. I'm always gone after the first night."

"I don't know what to say."

"Say it's wonderful."

"It's wonder...ful"

"Damn it, Carrie. Here." Mike took the glove off his right hand and pressed it to the glass window of the bookstore. "There must be a damn Bible in there somewhere. Carrie, I swear to you on a bookstore full of Bibles that I love you. I am coming back here for you. I swear, for God's Sake."

Carrie looked at the hand and then at Mike. She took her right mitten off and placed her hand on the window. "I swear on Roland's book, somewhere back in this store, that I love you, Michael and I will wait for you."

"Good."

"And I also swear I will hunt you down like a freaking dog if you don't"

It was a strange contract as contracts go, but it seemed to satisfy both parties. The bookstore oaths, in this case were quite binding. Mike and Carrie went back to her car and headed to the apartment above the meat market in Pipe to seal the deal.

Meg Bollander was startled in her dark living room, first by the crunch of tires coming into her turn-around drive and then by the flash of headlights across the wall. She wondered who on earth was coming to her house at this time of night. Only a few neighbors ever ventured on to her property and they were usually invited first. She quickly threw off the afghan and snapped on a light. She then when to the kitchen door just as someone knocked. She peeked out the window and saw Molly Costello.

"Land sake, girl, you scared the shit out of me," said Meg as she opened the door. "Get in here out of the cold night."

Molly looked a little sheepish, but she was smiling through it. "I knew you were up, Meg, and I figured you might like some company."

"You knew I was up?"

"I saw the lights on your little scooter thing when we drove in down there."

"You did?"

"Roland said you were probably planting explosives under the windmill."

"He said that, huh? Only good idea he ever had. You want a drink. I'm having one."

Molly saw what looked like another Old Fashion in Meg's hand. "Sure. Give me one of those." She started to sit down at the kitchen table, but Meg directed her into the living room. A minute later Meg handed her a drink.

"You must have something on your mind besides keeping me company," Meg said as she tidied up some books on the coffee table. Molly noticed one of them was Roland's.

"Actually, Meg, I feel like a bit of a rat coming up here. Roland didn't feel well, I think, and went to bed. The girls were exhausted and went right to bed, too. I was going to go over my notes before I retired, but then I thought of running up here real quick."

"You figured out how to get to my driveway, huh?"

"Wasn't that hard. I just kept my eye on the flashing light on the turbine and circled it until I found your mailbox. Bollander."

"You're pretty smart, but there are more Bollander's than cows around here."

"Maybe not enough, though, huh?"

It took Meg only a second to pick up Molly's drift. "You got his story today, huh? About him and my sister?"

"I got his side and, you know it was exactly like your story only with more detail."

"Well, that's good for you and your article, but I don't want to hear no more about it."

"You mad I came by?"

"No, honey, just no sense hashing it over, that's all."

"Well, I understand you feeling that way, but I thought maybe I could ask you just one question."

"Just one?"

"One."

"Okay, shoot."

"Do you ever talk to your sister?" Molly waited for the answer. She sipped her drink.

"She don't communicate back here anymore. When she left she left the whole damned bunch of us behind. Family, friends, everyone. No one has ever been more gone than her."

"I'm sorry, Meg."

"Me, too. Bet you didn't hear a sorry out of him, though, did you?"

Molly set her drink down and crossed her legs while leaning forward. It was a body language gesture indicating she wanted to be listened to carefully. "He didn't say the word, but it was there."

"Hrumph!"

"No Meg, it was more like him being sorry wasn't worth anything now. He understands what he did, but he can't undo it."

"That's the goddamned truth!"

"Meg, I think the man who did those things to you and your sister is living in the hell that you want him to be roasting in. But, here's the tricky part. The man he is today, the man who wrote those books, arose from that hell. He says he uninvented it and I believe him. What I need to learn is how such a thing is done."

"Sounds pretty schizo to me. Men aren't like that, Molly. They'll invent anything to get off the hook."

"Some do." Molly let those word dangle in the air.

Meg shook her ice cubes around her glass and sewered the rest of the drink. When she set the glass down she leveled her gaze at Molly with the precision of a laser. "I told you before, you find out how he did it with his writing. That is something I could see with my own eyes. If that ties in with your other theory I may give you a hearing on it. You think I got a closed mind, don't you? Well, honey, it is closed like the jaws of a snapping turtle on a stick. But, maybe you should consider this. I know something that you haven't figured out yet."

"What's that?'

Meg walked to the window and took a quick glance at the blinking red light atop the wind turbine across her field and then turned back to Molly, who might have been holding her breath.

"Garnet Granger *is* Roland Heinz."

Molly looked in on the girls, who were sleeping in what was still designated as 'Mike's room' even though Mike had yet to spend a night there. The room was chilly, like the rest of the upstairs, but the bed featured an awesome heavy quilt that Molly had pegged as antique and valuable. The girls looked warm and fast asleep. She stood for a moment as the shaft of pale light fell on the bed and felt that inner peace that a mother gets from watching her children sleep.

Melanie and Sonia had been adopted within a year of each other from the same international agency. Both were orphans and had been since being very young. They had little or no memory of who they were before the church people took them in. Melanie did have some dreams about a vague mother figure, but had attached herself so strongly to Molly that the dreams had faded. Sonia, who was of mixed African and Arab blood, was totally oblivious of her earliest history.

Molly's friends had warned her that the adoptions would all but insure that no man would be entering her life. She thought they were extreme views at the time, but now reality was proving them true. She had dated some interesting men, but they came and went quickly. Even the extremely liberal dates had not stuck around long enough to get to know Molly in the context of adoptive mother. She was perplexed at first and then acceptive. She loved the girls with all her heart and her work filled in the cracks. Perhaps, Roland and the other planets orbiting Ghost Farm had filled a crack or two also. As she closed the door and went across the hall to her own room, the expansiveness of that endearing thought flooded her mind with sleepy peace.

She got into bed and picked up *The Tap Root*, wanting to speed up her reading and find out what Meg had meant by her statement about the main character. Molly had read *A Winter Light* first and now that seemed like a mistake. The one being the sequel to the other; a sequel with more than a decade and a half between them. She wondered if she could decode Roland through Garnet Granger. She soon realized she was too sleepy to dig that deep tonight and fell asleep with the light on and the book on her stomach.

CHAPTER EIGHTEEN

I found Native American artifacts on the grounds over the years I have lived here at Ghost Farm. Mostly points, but once I found a grave. I could not be sure about who the person was or when he died so I had to call the Sheriff's Office. They informed me that it was a native site and put me in touch with an archeologist from the University of Wisconsin in Madison. This fellow and some of his students came up here and made a fine show of scientific procedure, carefully examining the skeleton and taking samples of DNA and clothing fibers. All in all, it was quite an interesting thing to observe. Ultimately, they went their way and I never did learn what exactly their findings were. I was supposed to get a report, but it never came. The body was reburied as near to the way I found it as was possible. I understood that part of it. What always mystified me was why it fell to me to discover him. Why, years after the end of his life, he came to cross my own. Then one autumn day in Brothertown, I met an Indian sitting outside the gas station. Nice looking young man with beautiful hair in a braid. He asked me if I was going into Fond du Lac because he needed a ride. He said he was going to his uncle's funeral at the Stanhope Funeral Home. He seemed familiar to me so I drove him in, waited and drove him back. When we shook hands I made the connection.

At some point during the night, Molly was aware that the light she had been reading by had been turned off. She felt for the book, but it was now off her stomach and on the blanket next to her. She was barely awake and laying very still when she felt the bed move and heard it make its tell-tale rusty creak. Someone had sat down on the end of the bed and she assumed it was one of the girls, but this woke her up a little more and quickly she knew something was wrong. She opened her eyes and saw a shadowy figure, lit only by the starlight coming in the window. She knew it was Roland.

"Roland, are you okay?" She started to reach for the light switch.

"Leave it dark, Molly."

"Is something wrong? Are you sick?" Molly was sitting up now, trying to adjust her eyes. She felt Roland's hand pat her foot.

"I'm okay. Maybe a little anxious. I'm sorry to come in here and wake you, but I need to talk to you, Molly."

"Can I turn on the light now?"

"No, I want to talk in the dark," Roland spoke softly. "I want to tell you about the, you know, the uninvented hell."

Molly had a thought that she banished in a second about asking him to wait until morning, sometime when she was alert and more prepared; but she considered that this moment might never come again. She leaned over to the table next to the bed and found her tape recorder. In the dark she felt the buttons and pressed 'Record.'

"You always have to use that thing?" asked Roland. His invisible frown was easy to imagine.

"It's a crutch, I know, but I rely on it. You can start talking anytime."

Roland paused for what seemed like an eternity. Molly thought he might change his mind and leave the room as ghostly as he had come into it. Then he cleared his throat and began to speak. His voice was almost ethereal. His brain was turning his concise and secret thoughts into words. Some time later, as the first and faintest shades of morning began to light the wallpaper, he finished and left the room. Molly turned off the recorder and held it tight. She had it! She had what she had come for, what Harry Stompe had sent her here for. She had what Meg raged to know. She had the keys to both the Pulitzer books. She was excited, but for some reason with that excitement came a deep sense of relief and she put her head down on the old down pillow and fell back asleep. She went immediately into a dream within a dream.

When Molly woke up she did indeed wonder if she had dreamt the whole thing. The recorder quickly confirmed that she did not. For a moment before rolling out of bed she lay there and studied the wallpaper patterns. They were corn-flowers by rail fences, repeated over and over and over from floor to ceiling and corner to corner. No one made wallpaper like that anymore, she thought. She had noticed the pattern before, but had not taken the time to appreciate its simple beauty. 'Amazing' was the word in her head. And then she wondered where the girls were. It was too quiet in the house.

Molly was surprised to see Carrie and Mike sitting at the kitchen table, but even more surprised that neither the girls nor Roland were there.

"Hi sleeping beauty," said Mike. "We've been waiting for you."

"I had a midnight visitor. Hi, Carrie." Molly stretched and yawned.

"Hi," smiled Carrie. "You look like you could use some coffee." She handed Molly a steaming cup. Oddly, it had the same pattern as the wallpaper. She looked at the dishes on the table and they all had the pattern that she had never noticed until now.

"Where are the girls? Where's Roland?" Molly asked, nodding thanks to Carrie.

"Well," said Mike, "They are all out in the barn watching some owl."

"An owl?"

"It's so cute," Carrie inserted. "The three of them are sitting in lawn chairs watching this owl that is watching them. I don't get it, but they do."

"I wonder if I should disturb them."

"Go ahead," said Mike. "I was out there taking pictures and none of them flinched. Owl included."

Molly started toward the door, but turned. "Sorry to bring this up again, but when are you leaving?" She addressed Mike, but looked for a wound in Carrie's face and didn't see one. Interesting, she thought.

"I got a flight tomorrow night," he said without emotion.

Molly nodded, but she was thinking, holy shit, these two have got it worked out. Maybe the week long romance was going to last. There were signs last night at dinner, but who knew what was going through their minds. This morning they both were calm and resolved. Love would always be a mystery to Molly, but she was damned impressed by this apparent example of it.

"I have one more photo op with him later. Some place special according to Roland."

"Okay, good. We can talk later."

Molly took her coffee and went out to the barn. The day was another bright stunner, but it didn't feel as cold as before. She noticed a great silver circle around the sun and knew that meant the weather was going to change yet again. She entered the darkened barn and saw the three chairs lined up with three of her favorite people sitting in them.

"Hoot, hoot," Molly said softly.

"Shhh, Mom," scolded Melanie.

"So sorry." Molly looked around but couldn't see the bird at first, but then she saw it on a rafter staring back at her like the intruder she obviously was. She walked up behind Sonia and whispered in her ear. "What are we doing?"

"Papa says we are riding through space with the owl," Sonia answered matter-of-factly.

"Sounds right to me." She then leaned into Roland. "Can we have a word outside?"

Roland nodded and they went back out into the light. The girls stayed in place, transfixed on the bird.

In the yard Molly faced Roland. "That was quite a night. How are you feeling today?"

He scratched his neck and squinted at the sun. "I've felt better, but I am glad to get that story out of the way. It was important."

"You worry me, Roland. All this urgency. Be honest with me."

"You have been getting heavy doses of honesty from me, girl." He paused. "But, you want to know about my health, correct?"

Molly nodded and waited.

"Shit, turn off the x-ray eyes, Molly. None of us know how much time we have left."

"Nice dodge."

"Okay, okay, I feel like shit, but I have days like this more often than not. You just gotta keep going that's all. The damned curtain will come down when the play is over."

"I'm worried that you are not going to tell me if you need to go to the hospital."

"I don't need to go. Yet."

"Then you will tell me?"

"Maybe."

Molly scowled.

"Okay, I'll tell you...unless I'm dead already."

Another scowl.

"Jesus, Mary, and Saint Joseph, Molly Costello, lighten up. I don't want those girls picking up on any of this."

"They are smarter and more perceptive than you think. They nail me all the time."

"Look, it's a nice day. I ain't gonna die today. We have work to finish. Mike has some work to finish. Did he tell you he is leaving tomorrow?"

"He did."

"So we are all building to the big climax. Those kids in the house, Mike and Carrie are probably more worried about tomorrow than I will ever be."

"Those kids, as you call them, are rock solid. I think they really have found something. And all in a week."

Roland leaned into Molly and put his arm around her. "One week. Do you believe what has happened in such a short amount of time? You know, this may have been the best week of my life."

"It has been special. The kids...we all love it here."

"Then let's just keep marching. There is a tide, you know, and it cannot be stayed."

"How about breakfast before philosophy?"

"I already ate."

"What did you eat?"

"Had a mouse in the barn about a half hour ago."

"You're loony."

"That, too.

"I love you, Roland."

Roland squeezed her and nodded before he broke away. He yelled for the girls in the barn and they came running out. All four of them went into the house, where Carrie was making cinnamon toast.

Harry Stompe was manning his desk at *Art Harvest* on Saturday morning. He liked working on the weekend when most of the staff was away. He also liked being in downtown Boston on a Saturday when his wife had a long list of chores for him to do at home in Chelmsford. He was reading emails and drinking coffee when a new email announced itself. It was from Mike Gabler and he could tell that the file was huge. Lots of pictures, he figured and as he opened it up, he knew he was correct. This email was followed quickly by five more. Yes, lots of pictures.

Harry got himself a coffee refill and hunted up a cup of yogurt from his mini-fridge. Then he began opening the files and scanning the fruit of Mike's work. He enlarged the thumbnails one by one and studied them. Some quickly and some with great concentration. The work was excellent as usual. There were hundreds of shots of his old friend Roland and a few of Molly, her girls, and some other folks he didn't recognize. One was a strikingly beautiful blonde. Local yokels, he figured. Background color. The last file contained the digital portraits that Mike had shot for the magazine cover. Harry pored over these with extreme concentration. He played with the tools in photo suite and did a little framing and experimental tricking. One picture was the most interesting to him. The lighting had been pretty even and regular in most of the shots, but there was one that had some sort of odd lighting effect. It looked like a bright flash, perhaps a reflection from outside the window Mike was getting his sunlight from. The result was eerie. A slash of light had been caught crossing Roland's face at a slight angle. It went directly across his eyes.

Harry zoomed in on this one shot and the results were astounding. Roland's eyes were revealed by the phantom light in a way that dramatized the intensity. Harry searched his mind for a word or two to describe what he saw, but could not come up with anything except the word 'divine.' Yes, he thought to himself, the eyes have a divine light. He flicked through a couple other thumbnails, but kept coming back to the strange picture. He could not decide if he loved it or it was too damned weird. All he knew was that it was extraordinary. He picked up his phone and dialed Mike Gabler's cell phone. Mike picked up the call right away.

"Mike here."

"Mike, it's Harry Stompe. Good morning"

"Oh, hi Harry. Mornin' to you, too. What's up?"

"Just got your emails and I love everything so far. Very nice work, Mike."

"Thanks. I'm just about finished. The other proofs are going to be in this afternoon and I will bring those back to Boston with me. I am flying back tomorrow and will drop them off on Monday. I have another shoot, you know."

"I know. Hey, I wanted to ask you about one of these pictures. It's in the last file you sent me with the cover portraits. The one with the crazy light on Roland's eyes. How did you do that?"

"I know the one you're talking about. Crazy is right. That flash was caused by Molly's car coming into the driveway. The sun off the windshield. It is one in a hundred million shot that the light would hit Roland's face just as I shot it. That it would light his eyes like that is bizarre. What do you think?"

"Not sure. What do you think, Mike?"

There was a three second pause before Mike answered. "I think it is the cover, Harry."

Now there was a five second pause. "Me, too."

"The light didn't wreck the shot, it created it," said Mike.

"I agree. Listen, is Molly there by any chance?"

"She's upstairs getting dressed."

"Okay, I'll talk to her later. How's Roland doing?"

"He seems okay. Maybe a little tired from all the company."

"He getting along with the girls?"

"Oh, heck, Harry, they love each other. They're already calling him Papa."

"No shit. Everything else okay?"

"Peachy."

"Who's the blonde, Mike?"

"She's sitting right here. You wanna talk to her?"

"Uh, no. You just answered my question."

CHAPTER NINETEEN

Crocus, daffodils, tulips, violets, forsythia, lilacs, phlox, clover, trillium, wild rose, tiger lilies, daisies, cornflowers, Queen Anne's lace, marsh orchids, purple aster, and then more cornflowers. Amen. The Midwesterner fingers rosary beads of bulbs, bushes, and wild flowers, every prayer answered in turn as the sun soars higher in the sky. They are the calendar of color, the names of heartstrings. They are the bouquets picked for Mom and the secret places where the bees make love. They are the feeding wands of birds and the wingless mirrors of butterflies. They are rewards for waiting out the long dark nights and the prisms that break down a winter light and turn it into summer lightning. My favorite is the cornflower, a true blue friend and the last stick to fall over in late Autumn. When I went looking for a place to live and work with my first real royalties, I was down to choosing between two farms. It seems the one I bought was already chosen for me by the previous owners. Not only were the old estate dishes in cornflower print, but also their bedroom wallpaper was a perfect match to the service. The wallpaper is faded and the dishes are chipped, but they will still be true blue long after I am gray dust.

By late morning Roland found himself alone. Mike and Carrie had gone into town to pick up his proofs at the photo lab and Molly and girls had gone to a local cheese factory outlet to buy some cheese to take home with them. Both of these errands served to remind him that the magical week was coming to a close. He wandered around the house, still delighting in the signs of his guests. There were still the opened suitcases on the floors of the bedrooms. Wet towels hung in the bathroom. The girl's bed was unmade and he sat down on it and ran his hands over the flannel sheets. It would be very hard saying goodbye to Melanie and Sonia. He had never spent much time around kids and not having any of his own was an old ache, but that was something he had left on the other side of the needle's eye.

That thought made him go into Molly's room, his room that he rarely used. Molly had made the bed, but there were notebooks, copies of his books, and odd pieces of paper strewn across the comforter. Roland spotted the tape recorder on the bedside table. He was drawn to it. Inside was his voice telling Molly things he had rarely even told to himself. He didn't like handling the machine for fear of ruining something, but he was compelled to do it just this once. He first pressed rewind and found that it already was cued. He then pressed play. He listened to his own voice as he looked out the window at the first flurries of a late morning snow squall.

I had bottomed out, Molly. Way past sink or swim. I was standing at the bottom of the ocean and about to let out the scream that would have drown me forever. The house I rented in Chilton was a mess. I could barely afford food, but I did manage to walk down to the gas station and get a six pack once or twice a day. I already told you about my little trip to Iowa. Soon I lost interest even in simple living and began to sleep more and more. The bottom rung of depression. No one ever came over and I didn't have a phone so the long spiral down was uninterrupted. Until the morning that I heard that dog barking in my front yard.

When the dog came into my life there was a not too subtle shift in my priorities. I had to feed the dog, right (?) so I needed to eliminate something else from my limited budget. I quit drinking. I see I have your raised eyebrow again. How could a dedicated alcoholic walk away from the urge? Well, it happened in the blink of an eye. The dog's eye.

Like I said ,I called her Sorry and she was a female. If whoever sent her to me had sent a male things might have been different. There was a look in her eye of compassion mixed with maternal care. What do you call it...nurturing? She also had a guilt-inducing gaze. Every time I turned around there she was, staring at me. One day I sat in a chair and she came over and sat right in front of me. I looked into those dark eyes and an idea began to hatch in my mind. I wondered what the heck she was looking at. I saw a gentle animal, but maybe she saw some titan or god trapped in his own creation, waist deep in hell.

And then I took it deeper. I went to the bathroom mirror and beheld the trapped god. I saw a billion years of stardust gathered in flesh. I saw a million years of tribal hate. I saw thousands of years of religious captivity. I saw hundreds of years of industrial clutter. I saw decades of addiction. I saw years of self-pity. I saw minutes of fear, I saw seconds of suicidal fixes. And then I saw the solution in a nano-second of blinding light. I saw the needle's eye I would need to pass through. My get-out-of-hell-free card. And remember, Molly, if this all sounds crazy, it was. I was about ninety-nine percent chemical back then. My head was only functioning on a cellular level. I needed a life raft. First it was the dog, then it was the book.

The Tap Root had no title then, just a concept. If we are all creations of some deity then we must be able to create the divine ourselves. I had to go back and uninvent all those things that I could not change. Please try to follow me, Molly. It's so important. If you become the character in your book, give her a worse life than your own, and then show her the way out of hell you can work the magic on yourself. I did it. You could do it, too. It's all in books. In writing.

Man alone has the intellect to write. He has written down every concept that he can conceptualize. He has used this gift for great good, but often greater ill. All of our ideas running loose looking for a page and then maybe finding a reader to believe the words. Words are the blood of the book. The book is the body of the imagination. The imagination is the soul of the writer. Where did this undying flame come from? If you say God, you are correct. But, if you say it comes from the writer, you would be correct, too. There is no difference. None. The author is the god of the book he is writing. My god first damned Garnet Granger...and then he saved her.

Roland heard the opening and the closing of the kitchen door downstairs and the sounds of the girls and Molly coming home. He quickly switched off the tape recorder and set it aside There were several more minutes of his speaking, he knew, but he had heard enough to know he had done pretty well with his explanation. He did wonder though, if Molly really understood.. A moment later he heard Sonia bounding up the stairs.

"Papa, Papa. Where are you, Papa?"

"In here, Sony." He had picked up Melanie's nickname for her sister. It seemed to stick with him. She hopped up onto the bed.

"We bought lots of cheese, Papa. Do you like cheese?"

"It's in my DNA."

"That means yes, right?"

"Yes."

Sonia looked around and then pounced on the copy of *A Winter Light* lying near the pillow. She immediately turned to the inside back dust cover photo of Roland and tapped it with her finger.

"This is you when you were young."

"Yes, dear, much younger."

"I like you better now," she stated with great certainty.

"Me, too."

"Mom says you are a great writer. Did you know I want to be a writer, too, when I get older? I can do that, right Papa?"

"Sony, there is a great writer in all of us. Some people can find his voice and others can't. It's like a gift."

Sonia nodded and snuggled into Roland. He could smell the scent of avocado in her soft hair.

"What is the name of the man inside you, Papa?"

"Some call him The Swift Sure Hand."

"Oh, because he can write real fast, huh?"

"Yes, something like that."

"I want to write books like *Harry Potter*," she stated while playing with Roland's fingers.

"That would be just fine, honey. People like to read exciting stories."

"What do you write about?"

"I try to make readers think about life. Mostly boring stuff like that."

"Carrie said she could not stop reading your book."

"It made her think."

"Oh."

Roland could tell Sonia was getting confused. He stood up and stretched.

"You go down and tell your mom I'm hungry. I'll be right down. Okay?"

"'Kay." Sonia bounded off, clumping down the stairs yelling that Papa was hungry and wanted some cheese.

Roland listened and smiled. He then went to the closet and opened it. On the top shelf in the back were four old fashioned hat boxes. Three of them still had the ornate hats of their day in them. One of the hat boxes had a treasure that would need to be opened soon.

Later when the girls were doing the lunch dishes and Molly was on the phone with the airlines, Mike came back in and plopped down next to Roland at the kitchen table. He had snow in his hair and on his shoulders, but he was smiling that certain smile.

"Hi girls."

Melanie and Sonia turned from the dishes and waved soapy hands. They were busy.

"It's starting to pile up out there, Roland," Mike said as he took off his jacket and hung it on the back of a chair.

"Oh, this ain't nothing," said Roland. "This little sun shower will be over in an hour."

"I don't know about that."

"I do. We have one last photo session."

"I have plenty of material already if we get snowed out, Roland." He paused and continued. "Besides, since when do you like getting your picture taken?"

"It's not so much the pictures, Mike. There is something I want to show you..." Roland glanced toward the girls. "And I need to talk to you, too."

"When?"

"Like I said, in about an hour."

"Okay, in the meantime I am going to take a nap."

"Go on out to the studio. No one will disturb you there. I'll come and get you in an hour. Okay?"

Mike waved and nodded as he grabbed his jacket and went out the back door. Roland walked over to the sink and tickled Melanie and she dropped a plate into the water, splashing Sonia. It started a giggle session that he was happy to have instigated. No one, but him noticed the involuntary shaking that his right hand was doing as it hung limp by his side. Roland also felt a drop of sweat roll down behind his left ear, which was ringing loudly. He quickly shook it all off.

CHAPTER TWENTY

I never collected a personal library. Many readers and some writers like to surround themselves with volumes; full shelves in cabinets and walls. Personally, I never saw a home library that looked used, but then I have not seen that many around here at all. I learned early, partly because my family had little extra money, that the library was the cheap way to build up one's reading muscle. I also always felt a certain sense of awe at the public library. I was overwhelmed with the idea that such wealth was assembled for the pleasure of everyone. I still have my first library card in my wallet. It's been through the wash a time or two, but I treasure it as an artifact of my youth. In our local library there is an aisle that has about a seven books, side by side, with my name printed on the spine. The last two books are duplicated, which is flattering, but I have never visited my aisle and shelf and found any of them checked out. I used to wonder if I had missed the mark, shot just wide of the target of popularity. But, then one day I was in that aisle when a distinguished woman of middle age walked directly to the shelf and pulled out one of my books and then just as quickly walked away to check it out. In all my literary career, I don't think I ever got a rush of pride or gratitude to rival that moment. It was as if she walked out of the library with my heart tucked under her arm.

"You've had quite a week, I'd say," said Pat Stirling as she exhaled her cigarette at Carrie's kitchen table. "When do I get to meet this guy, honey?"

"Mom, you can meet him when he comes back here next time." Carrie made the statement without a trace of wistfulness. Her mom noticed.

"And you're sure he is coming back. I mean you sound sure, Carrie."

Carrie edged her chair back and stood up. She disappeared into her bedroom for a second and then came back to the kitchen. She had a book in her hand and she placed it on the table in front of her mother.

"A week ago you came over here and gave me this book. Why?"

Pat placed her right hand on the book like she was about to take an oath while her left hand squashed the cigarette in an ashtray. Again she exhaled over her shoulder. "I read it and thought you might get something out of it."

"I did."

"You read this in a week? Wow. What did you think?"

"You were right. But, why exactly did you give it to me, Mom?"

"You might not like what I tell you."

"Go ahead. I think I already know, but I want to hear it."

"Well, the girl in the book, Garnet, well, in a way she reminded me of you. Not the part about being obese, of course, but the part about being trapped. She was trapped inside herself just like you are trapped inside your lifestyle. I guess I thought Heinz had a clearer, softer way of telling you some things I wanted to say."

"I got that part. And you're right, but gee, Mom, it was the timing. I started reading it and then Mike showed up to take pictures of Roland Heinz. Such a coincidence. Did you know anything about the magazine coming here to write about him?"

"No, honey. And I almost didn't even bring the book with me. I thought you might take it the wrong way. Like you often do with me."

"Oh, Mom."

"No, listen to me. There was the message, but then there were the words, too. I got dizzy reading this book. I have never read something so beautiful. It was more than a reading experience, it was like, I don't know, like dreaming Garnet Granger's dreams."

Carrie gave her hand a wave to get the last string of lingering smoke away from her and smiled. "You are way deeper than I thought, Mom. I had the same kind of feeling. Okay, now it's my turn." She got up again and opened a drawer in a small table by the window. She took out a copy of *A Winter Light* and placed it front of Pat.

"It's signed by the author to you personally."

"No shit?" Pat said as she opened the cover and read the dedication. Then she grasped it in both hands and seemed to weigh it.

"Pulitzer number two, Mom. The further adventures of Garnet Granger."

Pat looked at Carrie and then the book, shaking her head. "But the girl died in the first book."

"Yeah, she sure did," said Carrie." I think you have some more reading to do."

Roland took two pairs of snowshoes off their hooks inside the barn door and handed one pair to Mike.

"You ever used these things?" he asked.

"No."

"Well, these modern ones are easier to use than the old ones you used to have to strap on. These snap on like skis. They both sat down on a bench and put on the odd shoes. Mike stood up and tested the feel.

"And this is going to make walking easier?"

"Yep. Better to walk on top of this fresh snow than to trudge through it. Com'on."

The two men headed off out of the barn and made for the southeast corner of Roland's property where a large grove of barren trees loomed. The snow was letting up now, but the sky was still low and leaden. Mike carried only a small, lightweight tripod and a small camera bag. He held little hope for photographing anything too interesting in this dull light, but he was enjoying the walk.

When they reached the grove of trees, Mike followed as Roland led them deeper into the stark woods. They went in single file and Mike noticed all sorts of animal tracks already in the fresh snow. There were more birds than he thought there would be in this forest without leaves. Even the bright red flash of a pair of cardinals caught his eye. Mostly, he heard the caw of crows coming from somewhere up ahead. In a few more minutes of walking they had circled back a little west and reached an outcropping of limestone at the edge of the trees. They were now on The Ledge.

Roland found a fallen tree that made a natural bench and sat down. Mike set his gear down and did the same. As if on cue, there was a hole in the clouds opening above them and blue sky could be seen within it. A breeze picked up and the hole widened quickly as the woods began to take on a new light. Roland turned to Mike and punched his arm.

"See, I told you the squall would stop just in time."

"Right as usual, Roland. I take it you come here often, eh?"

"Well, maybe not often enough. This here is my favorite place to come on a late winter afternoon. It inspires me. Let's give it a minute or two."

Roland then produced a small flask from his jacket and handed it to Mike.

"What is it?' Mike asked out of habit. He didn't really care as long as it was strong.

"Just some blackberry brandy. Goes good with the snow."

Mike nodded unknowingly and took a swallow. He handed it back to Roland, who took a quick sip. The light was changing rapidly now as the sun was starting to reveal itself behind a veil of disappearing clouds. When the first salmon pink hues hit the fresh snow Mike got the camera out and on to the tripod. He told Roland to stay where he was as he moved to the edge of the outcropping and let the light begin to fill Roland's face. He was using the bigger digital camera. He didn't want to mess with film changing or any more photo labs. He was shooting rapid fire as the light was fading fast. Soon the pink was turning to amethyst, and a dozen other shades of purple.

"This is the light I like," said Roland. "This is what I wanted you to get."

"Oh?"

"You know, Mike, for Harry Stompe's posthumous book. I figured that out a long time ago."

Mike smiled and kept shooting until the light was gone.

"That's it, Roland. Not enough light now."

"Okay, but sit down here for a minute."

The sun was now just below the horizon across the vast expanse of Lake Winnebago and the stars were beginning to pop out overhead. The temperature was dropping rapidly, but the wind had gone down to dead calm. The crows were silent now and there was no sound except for the soft breathing of the men.

"I wanted to tell you a couple things, Mike." Roland took the flask back out and handed it Mike. Here, put this in your pocket."

Mike shrugged, but obeyed.

"First of all, thanks for being patient with me this week," Roland began. "I never liked having my picture taken, but you made it interesting and fun."

Mike decided to just listen. He knew this was leading up to something else.

"There is a hat box on the shelf in the closet in my room. The room Molly is using. There is something in that box that I want you to give to her in case....well. I want you to know it's there, okay?"

Mike nodded, but decided to remain silent and listen.

"I'm not feeling too hot today. It makes me realize that...well, my time is running out. It's okay. God, I have been running on fumes for the last three or four months. Anyway, I really wanted to get up here one more time. This is my spot. The Ledge is like the proverbial end of the earth. Everything behind me is dark and everything out there," he pointed to the afterglow, "is what's ahead. You gonna say anything?"

"I was letting you speak."

"Well, I want to hear your voice, too. Tell me about what you and the girl are going to do."

"Well, the only firm plan we have is to never let this end. This, whatever it was that happened."

"Hah, she got you, huh?" I told you about Wisconsin girls. Well, good for both of you. Sometimes the magic happens when you least expect it. That's why they call it magic."

"I always thought it would be like, I don't know, like a loud explosion in the heart. Turns out *it is the thinnest blade of calm, quiet like a winter light."* Mike turned to Roland and smiled.

"So you're stealing my lines now, huh?"

"Carrie and I have been reading both books."

Roland stood up and smiled. Let's go back and see what the girls are up to."

Mike grabbed his gear and followed Roland back to Ghost Farm as a full moon rose over The Ledge. They didn't quite make it back to the farm before Roland collapsed in the snow.

Meg Bollander had watched the lovely winter sunset from her usual perch. She was in her chair facing the lake with the afghan over her legs. She was thinking about the old Frank Sinatra song, *Saturday Night is the Loneliest Night of the Week.* It wasn't the first time it had run through her head. She figured she had two choices. Either she could go to Saturday night mass in Johnsburg or go make a drink. Or she could do neither. Or she could do both. The early winter darkness was making her crazy again.

Before she could get herself motivated to do anything, the flashing lights of the ambulance caught her eye coming up Highway 151. It could have been heading anywhere, but she knew instinctively when it would slow down and where it would turn. She had watched the same scenario just a week ago. She had Molly's cell phone number now and could easily have made the call of a concerned neighbor, but dismissed the thought.

She watched as the minutes went by and then followed the ambulance as it headed back down the road to Fond du Lac. She saw a second set of headlights go back down the drive and follow the ambulance down the road. She watched for a little while longer and pondered the trouble that had headed off to the south. She decided to go to mass, but she'd be damned if she was going to pray for him.

Roland was conscious by the time the paramedics arrived, but in no condition to protest being hauled off to the hospital for the second straight Saturday night. Molly drove the van in behind the ambulance, while Mike waited for Carrie to arrive to watch the girls. He wanted to go to the hospital with Molly, but he couldn't reach Carrie right away. As it was, she had called back a couple minutes later and was heading over, but needed to find someone to work for her later. The girls were very upset that Papa was sick. The ambulance had scared them. It made the danger all too real; much more so than the appearance of Papa 'sleeping' in the snow.

When Carrie arrived Mike was out the door quickly, but not before their week old teamwork had kicked in. She knew her job was to distract the girls and he knew she would be perfect for doing it. Carrie had anticipated something like this and had grabbed a cake mix and the other necessary ingredients to get one in the oven with the girls help, of course. Baking and then icing the cake made the evening pass a little faster. It was going to be a long one, Carrie knew.

CHAPTER TWENTY-ONE

I grew up Roman Catholic and pretty much remained one throughout much of my life. I went from devout alter boy to a Christmas and Easter mass-goer as I grew older, but I could always still consider myself to be Catholic. Of course, that changed when I changed. After my personal epiphany, when I finally was 'saved' from drinking and its attendant self-loathing, I ironically found I no longer had any need for formal religion. I suppose this was all part of my process of uninvention, but I did take bits and pieces of the old parishioner and tied them in with the New Age alchemist. I found that by eliminating the middlemen of the church I was able to build a stronger relationship with the boss. I need to say here that I understand the relationship of the shepherd and his flock, but the occasional blackest of sheep will wander so far away that they never find their way back. Having done so, I had to rename the rituals and rephrase the liturgies to fit my personal grasp of who I was and what I meant to Him. I came to believe that every man and woman is the son and daughter of God. Some one once observed of me that I had 'grown so secular.' I shrugged and replied that at least I had grown.

Karl and Vi's Tap in Johnsburg looked too inviting for Meg to resist again after the speedy and efficient Saturday night mass. Besides, going home represented some sort of Saturday night defeat. It was the last and only choice she had and she did not enter the bar with any expectations of anything besides diversion. Diversion was sitting in her usual place, talons gripping the rail, and wearing what appeared to be the same clothes as almost a week ago. The hair curlers were gone, however, revealing a newly blued coif. Meg sat down next to Mrs. Dankermann.

"Hello again," began Meg as Mrs. Dankermann's head turned slowly to see who had addressed her.

"Hah, the Bollander girl returns. Hello yourself."

"Nice evening to be out on the local night club circuit."

The old woman took a swallow of her clear drink and then wiped her lips and teeth with the cocktail napkin. "You mean the shit hole circuit, don't you dear?"

Meg didn't know how to reply to the statement, although it was obviously true. She tried to change the subject. "How do you get here? Surely you don't drive...I mean." Meg had dug her own hole now.

"It's okay, dear. I stopped driving shortly after the automobile was invented." She chuckled at her own wit. "I just walk here and crawl home. I haunt that little white house across the street now."

"Oh, when did you move to Johnsburg?"

"Think Kennedy was president. Somewhere back there. Who can keep track of time these days?"

Meg pondered the profundity of the statement. Thankfully, the bartender finally got around to her and she ordered white wine. She bought Mrs. Dankermann whatever she was drinking, which was vodka on the rocks. The ladies sat silently for a few minutes as the bar hummed around them. The older lady broke the silence after the drinks came.

"You ever find out what happened to Rollie Heinz?"

Meg was startled at the old woman's memory and showed it with raised eyebrows.

"No, but I guess he was okay, but..."

"But what, dear?"

"Well, I think he went back to the hospital tonight," Meg said carefully. She didn't want to get into any Roland talk tonight.

"Well, I'd say if he had to get taken away twice in a week, he probably ain't coming home again," the old woman postulated. "Least that's my experience."

When Meg looked at Mrs. Dankermann just then she saw for the first time the cadaver-in-waiting that the old woman was. It was like sitting next to the Grim Reaper's ex wife and third cousin. She also saw very clearly what could be her own future.

"I suppose," Meg mumbled as a cold chill passed through her. Suddenly, she needed to be out of the bar and back home. If Mrs. Dankermann was going to be her social companion then she really didn't want one. Without another word she grabbed her purse and gave a weak good night wave. Outside the door she passed by the window long enough to see Mrs. Dankermann slide her untouched glass of wine over next to her vodka. As she drove home on the snowy roads, her panic went away slowly. It was replaced by another, duller ache. She sensed, like the old woman, that Roland was not coming home this time. Somehow, the possibility infuriated her.

At the ICU at St. Agnes Hospital Roland was holding his own. That's what the doctor told Molly, as she explained that she was not family, but a house guest. The doctor, understanding the obvious concern on Molly's face, still could not tell her much about Roland's specifics. He suggested she go home and leave her cell phone number with the nurse on duty. Molly was flustered, but understood the protocol. Mike arrived just as she was deciding what to do.

"How is he?" Molly was so glad to see Mike that she hugged him.

"He's in Intensive Care. The doc won't tell me much because I am not family. Jesus, Mike I sure feel like family."

"I know how you feel."

"How are the girls? They were so upset, especially Sony."

"Carrie is teaching them how to bake a cake. They are making it for Papa. You know."

Molly smiled at the vision. "Mike, I have to ask you, did you see any of this coming on when you guys went off into the woods?"

"Not really, but he was talking to me like he was making his peace a little. He said he wasn't feeling well, but didn't say it was more than any other day. But, he did give me some instructions."

"Like what?" Molly eyes darted across Mike's face searching for answers.

"He told me where something was that I am supposed to give to you if...when."

"If he dies? You can say it, Mike."

"Yeah. Look, Molly, I knew... you knew he was sick, but I still can't figure out if I wanted this to happen when I was still here or when I was gone. I've come to really care about that man."

"I had the same thoughts a few days ago, but now I so glad we are all still here. He is family now, Mike, even if the hospital doesn't recognize it. He is all of our Papa." With this, Molly began to cry and Mike led her to an area where there was some privacy and a couple of comfortable chairs. Molly sat down and found some Kleenex in her purse and put it to use.

"I called Harry on the way in," said Molly.

"And?"

"He's flying in tomorrow or Monday depending on flights. I told him to plan on staying at Roland's. Can you stay or are you still leaving tomorrow?"

"I have a call in to my clients for next week. We should be able to reschedule. This was not a deadline sort of job," Mike noted. He had never, ever cancelled a shoot before and was a little hesitant to do it, but he had felt the shift inside himself, too. Pipe, Wisconsin was now a like home with all the priorities that were included in that emotional change.

"Let's go home, Molly," he continued. There's nothing we can do for Roland hanging around here. Maybe they'll let us see him in the morning."

Molly had not been ready to leave, but saw the wisdom in Mike's assessment.

"I guess we should. The girls won't go to bed until I'm home and I don't want to make Carrie stay all night waiting for us."

"Carrie understands and told me to tell you that she would stay as long as we need her."

"She is just great, Mike. I am not sure I have told you how happy and jealous I am for you both."

"I like you happy and jealous, Molly Costello." He stood and gave her a warm smile. "Let's go home."

In the ICU, Roland Heinz was feeling pretty good. He assumed it was because of some drug. He hated all the monitoring equipment around him and the various tubes and wires connected to his body, but he had prepared for this night and felt a little detached. He knew that the road he was now irrevocably walking down led to the next needle's eye he needed to pass through. He'd get there eventually with or without the medical clutter around him. He soon drifted into sleep despite the beeps and whispers and quickly rolled his first dream into a second one.

With the protection of the second dream layer, Roland found himself standing in the quarry where he had worked for most of his married years. He looked around and he was quite alone. More than alone, the pit was quiet. This clue that it was a dream would normally have awakened him, but being in a state two dreams deep, he was able to justify the oddity and continue.

There was a clear blue sky overhead, not a cloud in sight. The dream did allow birds, as they often do, and a huge skein of a thousand geese raked the blue dome above him. He noted they were heading south so he fixed the time as Fall. At his feet was a wooden box marked 'Explosives' and he recognized the labeling. It seemed obvious he was there to blow something up. As he ritualistically prepared the charges and placed them in a hole in the rock face, he felt a familiar presence and turned to it. Karin was standing behind him holding a glass of iced tea. He took it from her and drank it, but it tasted first like sweet tea, then whiskey and then like blood. She gave him a kiss on the cheek and vanished.

Now the dream had sound. The geese were honking noisily overhead. He heard the trickle of dislodged rocks as he tamped the charge into the hole and wired up the detonator. Loose gravel crunched under his boots. He knew he was supposed to play out the wire and take cover behind the blast barrier, but he made no such move. Against his usual precautions, he stood by the blast hole and then did something he knew should not work, but it did anyway. He touched two wires together and the side of the rock face blew away. He expected immediate pain, but there was none. He expected to awaken, but he couldn't quite do it. Then as he slowly surfaced through the dream layers he knew he was back in the hospital, but he could not open his eyes. It took a tremendous effort to get his eyes open. He got panicky and forced his arm to move. The violent spasm sent an IV tube flying away from his arm and an alarm sounded on a monitor next to him. Roland opened his eyes and saw someone running towards him. Well, at least I am still alive he, thought to himself. Then he wondered if that was a good thing.

There was the smell of baking at Ghost Farm when Molly and Mike got back there. The girls were already sleepy and Molly got them off to bed, while Mike explained the new situation to Carrie. Carrie knew that Mike's postponement of departure was only temporary, but she was very relieved that he was not going to have to fly off right away and leave the women to sort it all out. While Molly was still up with the kids, Carrie decided to head home alone, figuring Mike and Molly had some planning to do; contingencies to address. Mike walked her out to her car where they held hands with their foreheads touching for several quiet minutes. When she left, Mike went inside and heard the house phone ringing. It was the ring of an old phone, deep and alarming. He had not heard it before and had a bad feeling about it. Especially at this time of night.

Molly, too, was startled by the phone as she got to the bottom of the steps. It hung on the wall in the kitchen and that is where she took a deep breath before answering it. Mike hovered.

"Hello?"

"Uh, hello, is this Molly Costello?'

It was a man's voice and Molly's heart began to shut down.

"Yes, it is."

"Ms. Costello, I'm sorry to be calling so late. This is Patrick Zaneb, Roland's attorney."

"Yes, hello, Mr. Zaneb?" Her mind was still not reassured, but at least it was not the hospital calling.

"I can tell by your voice that you might have been expecting some news about Roland. Sorry to startled you, but as far as I know he is resting comfortably right now."

"Thank you. We just came back from the hospital about a half hour ago and they wouldn't give us much information."

"Yes, of course, but that won't be a problem anymore."

Molly did a head cock that Mike picked up on. The gesture meant something interesting was happening. "What do you mean exactly?"

"Well," Patrick continued, "when I learned that he was back in the hospital I called the administrator at home. We are all old friends, and I explained that Roland had given you power of attorney."

"He did what?"

"Earlier this week Roland came to see me and we made some changes to his living will and other personal documents. One of them gives you power of attorney for Roland's affairs. And that includes his medical decisions so you are now considered to be equal to immediate family. The fact is that he has no other living family so you are it. Any problems?"

"Other than being flabbergasted, I don't have any. So I can see Roland in the morning?"

"Yes, any time you wish. And please call me after you see him."

Molly promised that she would do that and took Patrick's number. The she said goodbye and hung up. She turned to Mike.

"Did you get the gist of that?"

"Not really," said Mike.

"It was Roland's lawyer. As of a couple days ago, I have his power of attorney. What the heck is that all about?"

Mike thought for moment. "Actually, it makes perfect sense, Molly. I know from talking to him that he has no family. Who is closer to him than you?"

"My god, Mike, it's only been a week."

"How long does it seem though?"

Molly started to say something, but then she just shook her head. "Seems like forever," she admitted very softly. "I need to get some sleep. This is all too crazy right now. You staying here or you going over to Carrie's?"

"I'm staying here tonight. I'll be down here on the couch in case that phone rings again."

"Let's hope it doesn't, huh?"

Mike nodded. He extended his fist out toward Molly and she tapped it with hers. Solidarity before sleep. The night passed with the phone not ringing.

CHAPTER TWENTY-TWO

In the summer of '69 my marriage was still in tact although the seeds of its demise were already sown and being carefully irrigated by my drinking. Looking back perhaps the situation was as hopeless as I was blind, but there was one summer night that just might have turned things around. It was a Sunday night and Karin and I had spent the day at a Lake Michigan beach over near Two Rivers. I remember both of us being totally sun burnt so that we could feel the heat of the day on our skin long after the sun went down. On the way home to Fond du Lac we stopped at the scenic overlook on Highway 151 where it begins to spill down The Ledge north of Brothertown. I had a white Pontiac convertible that year, which was probably the last new car I ever owned. The top was down and I remember looking over at my wife, her head was back and her eyes were closed as if in rapture. We were both listening to the car radio, but there was no music on this July night. Every station within reach was broadcasting only news. It was July 20th and men were landing on that moon that was sitting right out there, hovering over Lake Winnebago. On a night when such a thing was not only possible, but actually happening in front of us, there were as many miracles in the air as fireflies. The complexity of science had made it to the first rung of the stairway to heaven. I imagined a new future for us. Then suddenly, Karin snapped off the radio and said that she wanted to go home. The moment was gone and I asked her what was wrong. She simply pointed at the moon. 'I don't believe anyone's up there', she said, and having said that we drove home about 240,000 miles apart.

Harry Stompe, aboard his flight from Logan to O'Hare, had just broken through the low snow clouds over western Massachusetts and the jet was suddenly glowing with morning sunshine in the cabin. The Sunday morning flight was mostly full, but Harry found the atmosphere to be pleasant despite the usual hum and chatter of confined humanity.

His mind turned to the night before. Molly's call had struck
him as slightly frantic considering the circumstances. After all,
she had only been in Wisconsin with Heinz for a week, but
there was an urgent plea that maybe he did understand. If
Roland had already adopted Molly and the girls; if he had
shown them his rare and intimate light, then he understood
completely. Roland had done as much to him many years ago
in Chicago. He closed his eyes and remembered.

Heinz was introduced to him by Chick Connell, who was
an Army buddy of Roland's. Chick was a novelist with some
potential in those days. He later switched to poetry, but that's
a different story. Harry was doing book reviews for the
Chicago Tribune and through them had come to know Connell. Harry had given Chick a tepid review of a long forgotten
title and now Chick, who Harry now considered a friend,
wanted him to meet this unpublished writer he knew. The
meeting, like most literary confabs of those days, took place
in a bar. This time it was The Billy Goat Tavern on Lower
Wacker Drive beneath The Tribune Tower. The place had
atmosphere if little else. Harry recalled the meeting was just
after the lunch crowd had cleared out and the place was
nearly empty. He got there early and then in walks Chick with
this big farmer-looking guy. Harry's first impression of Roland
Heinz was not a very good one. And yet, recalled, Harry,
there was something about Roland that he could not quite put
his finger on. Something about the flinty eyes that were taking
in every movement, every sound. Harry also noticed the deep
despair in those eyes. Something was injured inside this guy,
he thought. Something that was trying to get out. Perhaps he
could own some writer's instincts after all. Whatever it was he
liked the big oaf.

Drinks were ordered and reordered and eventually a
manuscript was produced, bound in three ring folder. It was
thick and heavy, which matched Harry's tongue by that point
in the day. He promised to read it and then went back to work.
The manuscript sat on his desk for nearly a month, unread.
Harry didn't remember taking it home, but one night he was
looking for something to read himself to sleep and picked it

up. He remembered the title, *The Kennel Klub*. It was a Viet Nam war saga with the narrative being told by a soldier to a hooker in a Saigon night club named by the title.

In the late '70's this sort of book's appeal was minimal due to the hangover and fatigue of the war. As a war story went, the work was not very exciting, but Harry did find a literary thread in the writing that made it quirky-interesting in his mind. In fact, he read it twice before calling a publisher he knew who was looking for some new talent. Ultimately, the book got a limited publishing under another title with heavy editing and a very small advance to Roland. Harry knew for a fact that Roland probably drank the advance within a week of getting it. The book went quickly to the throw-away tables in bookstores and then disappeared completely.

Harry accepted the fact that he had become Roland's de facto agent and managed to get two more of his books published; this time with no advance. The fact was that Harry never made a dime on Roland, but they did become friends and Harry did get valuable experience as an agent and later, a magazine editor. Roland was never his money maker, but he was his first client. Sadly, Roland's flashes of talent never went beyond a certain point. The three war novels covered too many of the same themes and the characters were stony. The writer and the adopted agent grew apart. Then they lost touch completely.

Harry sorted the story in his head as the plane softly droned its way west over the Great Lakes. He looked out his window and saw they were over water. He looked at his watch and guessed it was Lake Michigan meaning Chicago was not far away. At that moment there was an intercom bong and a flight attendant confirmed that they were now on approach to O'Hare. Harry realized he had dozed off while thinking about Roland and the old days. Closing his eyes again for the descent, he noted that those days of flop books and disconnect had ended abruptly one day in 1994 when a package arrived at his new office in Boston. It arrived just before Christmas like a present. He had just taken the position of Editor in Chief at *Art Harvest*, having finally found the money and security that newspapers and literary agency had never produced.

The package was a rough first draft manuscript of *The Tap Root*. At first he couldn't believe that Roland Heinz had produced this work, but after starting it he recognized the style. All the good traits that had been so rare in the war books were now great traits and splashing purple on every page. It was the most beautiful novel he had ever read. Now, what to do with it. He did not want to jeopardize his new position by veering off back into being an agent, but he knew he was holding solid gold in his hands. He tried to call Roland, but the number he had in his book was no longer in use. He eventually located the number in Pipe, Wisconsin, but still could not get a hold of Roland. This went on for days.

Harry had stayed in touch with Chick Connell, who was now C. M. Connell, the poet. Connell was a regular contributor to *Art Harvest*, so he was at least easy to find. Without any initial okay from Roland, Harry sent a copy of the manuscript to Connell, who passed it on to his publisher. A pending deal for the book was created a week before Roland could be located and told. It was not going to be a huge advance, but one worthy of the effort. Six months later it was reviewed in The New York Times Book Review and the rest, as they say, is history. Pulitzer number one. But, then history can be long. Seventeen years went by before *A Winter Light* came along. Nearly forgotten again and without warning, Roland Heinz reappeared back into the literary world with a bang. The sequel to *The Tap Root*, *A Winter Light* was so good, so fresh, and so desperately loved that it immediately got world attention. Bang, Pulitzer number two. Harry always wondered how Roland had done it. The person who found the answer to that mystery would make his or her own bones in the book biz. And then came the letter summoning Molly Costello to come get the interview. The first, only, and last interview. And it was going to run in his monthly.

Harry Stompe was an old friend, but he was also a businessman and entrepreneur. He wanted to be in on the solution to that mystery. He always suspected that there was going to be a revelation from Roland as his health declined. Now it was all happening and his writer, Molly was the key: Roland's chosen confessor.

The intercom bonged again and the passengers were told to get ready to land. Harry found his rental car information in his coat pocket and sat with his cell phone in his hand waiting for the attendant's permission to use it. At the gate finally, he dialed Molly. He got her at the hospital, where she handed the phone to Roland. His voice was weak, but he was lucid.

"Hey, Harry, hear you're coming up."

"How you doing, Roland?"

"It's getting interesting."

"What do you mean, interesting?"

"Aw, you'll find out someday, Harry. See you soon."

It sounded like Roland was trying to give the phone back to Molly, but it disconnected. Harry was suddenly very anxious to get out of his seat and begin his drive to Wisconsin.

Molly was refusing to enter the death watch mode. It was more than simple denial. She and Roland had been having a conversation for over an hour and he simply wasn't sounding or looking deathly. Of course, there was no doctor available on Sunday morning so she would have to wait for a prognosis, but just seeing Roland was cheering her. Even with his nasal oxygen cannula and puncture bruises on his arms, they were still covering ground for the story she would soon be writing.

"Roland, I still need to know about those years between the two novels. That was a long time and I know you could not have been wasting it."

Roland took a sip of water from a plastic cup with a cover and a straw. He closed his eyes as the water ran down into the core of his body. He followed the flow in his mind for a second in the caverns of his illness.

"Those years went by pretty fast, dear. I spent a lot of time inside Garnet Granger's head trying to figure out what came next. After all, she died right? What comes after death?'

It would have been a purely rhetorical question had he not been in Intensive Care with a monitor beeping and graphing his own heartbeats. He saw Molly's furrowed brow.

"Spare me the look, Molly. You've read the books. I surely don't need to explain them to you point by point. I understand there have been dozens of books written analyzing the character of Garnet."

"Most of those are psychology books. She has become a case study."

"Wish I had time to read them. Might be interesting to finally get shrunk all these years later."

"Meg clued me in on you and Garnet. She knew," said Molly looking for a reaction.

"Meg was always a pretty smart girl."

"She's no girl anymore, Roland."

"Hah, she stopped growing a long time ago when she started getting a taste for bitterness."

"You two should make your peace."

Roland was silent for a few moments then he looked Molly in the eye, which was how he prepped the truth. "The man she would make peace with no longer exists. She knows that. She could come into this room, hold my hand, and kiss my cheek and it wouldn't mean a damned thing. Maybe she could do that to the man who wrote those books, but she would know deep down that the other man wasn't in the room. He's the one she hates and cannot forgive."

"I think you're right."

"You think I'm right? It's a hard lesson to learn. Complex as hell. Like I always said, Molly, the best poems are the saddest."

A nurse quietly intruded and began to take Roland's blood pressure. She was cheery and efficient, which gave both Roland and Molly a chill. A technician had disturbed their voyage into the mind. When she was done Roland was suddenly tired, his eyelids falling.

"I'll let you take a nap," Molly whispered.

Roland's eyes fluttered and he smiled. "Okay. Come back later, okay?"

"I will."

Somewhat reluctantly, she left the bedside and wound her way back out to the lobby and out into the parking lot. When Molly got into the van and started it up, she put her head on to her hands atop the steering wheel and wept. Something clear had entered her head. Papa was almost finished living.

CHAPTER TWENTY-THREE

The only family record I retain is an old King James Bible that had a short genealogy section that someone, probably an aunt filled out many years ago. It only went as far back as my grandparents, whose names were Manfred Peter Heinz and Dorothy Cobb Heinz. Manny and Dot. Further history was passed along by word of mouth, snippets I picked up at family get-togethers. Manny came to Wisconsin following a brother, who was a farmer and he went to work for him near Kloten. It seemed that part of Wisconsin looked a lot like eastern Germany. I have never been there. Dot was considered a local girl, probably third generation Irish. I think I heard that she was the Catholic and Manny was Lutheran and she converted him before marriage. That's how it went back then. They had five kids, four girls and my dad, William Roland Heinz, who married Betty Hallstrom in 1934. My Dad died in a barn fire, that no one ever talked about, when I was nine and Mom passed the year I turned seventeen from pneumonia. I was an only child and by that time my aunts, uncles, and cousins were probably spread across the country like gypsies, except for one local cousin, Barb, whom I rarely see. I often wondered about what it would be like, how healthy it would be to just have a meal with folks of your own blood. Folks who shared the old family stories and gossip. I had to create my family within my stories. A lonely craft, indeed.

Harry Stompe's rental car had a GPS system, per his request, and it was now guiding him off of US Route 41 onto the Highway 151 Bypass around Fond du Lac. He noted the large blue mass at the top of his color display that denoted Lake Winnebago. Eventually, Pipe showed up on the display, but the address for Roland's farm was stumping the system. He pulled over at a place called The Little Farmer and dialed Molly's cell phone. She answered on the third ring.

"Hello, Harry, where are you?"

Harry knew she had his caller ID so he was not surprised. "I am close, but I can't find Roland's drive. I am at the Little Farmer."

"Oh, you're right down the road. Just drive north about another two miles. We're on the right side. I'll go down to the end of the drive and meet you."

A few minutes later Harry saw Molly waving and pulled into the drive. She got in and they went up the last hundred yards to the house. Once inside, Molly made coffee while Harry used the bathroom and dropped his suitcase in the room Mike never used.

It was now around 4 PM and Molly realized she would need to think about dinner. The girls and Mike were over at Carrie's place doing something fun she hoped. She had been intentionally protecting the girls from doting on Roland and his health. She knew the girls were worried, but diversion seemed to be working. She again thought about what a gem Carrie was and how she and Mike had teamed up to help everyone out. Now she turned her attention to her boss.

"Have a good trip out?" Molly asked as she handed Harry a mug of the fresh brewed coffee.

"It was just fine. Thanks, Molly," he said as he took the mug. "It gave me the time to do some thinking about Roland, you know the early days. He was always sort of out of focus for me back then."

"How so?"

"Well, the book crowd in Chicago back then was a bunch of serious party monsters. Roland was just plain old serious. When Roland came down to the city Chick Connell tried to work him into the group, but Roland never would lighten up. Oh, he could drink with the best of us, but it was never any fun for him. I eventually figured out that his marriage was pretty much shot up here. Stuff like that happens to everyone, but our buddy had an anvil around his heart. I helped him out a little getting some crap published, but I never saw anything big and bright in his crystal ball. Then he disappeared off the face of the earth.

"He's told me what a mess he was back then, but you know, you're right. Lots of people go through bad marriages, alcohol abuse, even the domestic violence, but Roland went to a very bad place for a very long time," Molly added.

"I guess it was from that place that he began to write the good stuff."

"Uh, uh, no, Harry" Molly shook her head. "It was after he left the bad place. In his own words he turned his skin inside out and shed it."

Harry nodded and looked at Molly as if seeing her for the first time. "You figured it out, haven't you? You know the how, when, what, and why of how he wrote those two books."

"That's what you sent me her for, right?"

Harry nodded and looked far away into his coffee mug. "Did he write them here?"

"He wrote *The Tap Root* at some rented house in Chilton. Up the road a ways. He wrote *A Winter Light* in that shed just outside there. He bought this place with his first royalties and prize money."

Harry stood and walked to the window and peered out locating the old cheese shed. "You know, Molly, I am just enough of a book lover to get goose bumps just being here. This place has a certain feel to it. Like something great happened here."

"It did."

Harry turned back to her. "Yes, it did. Which makes me wonder all the more what happened during those years between the books. Something is missing. Did you ask him?"

"Of course I did, but he was vague. You could almost say mysterious. Anyway, that's the feeling I got."

"So you think he wrote during that period?"

It was now Molly's turn to look hard at Harry. She thought she saw something she didn't quite like. "Harry, I have to ask, did you come here to see and old friend or did you come looking for buried treasure?"

Harry smiled. "You're good. Do you read everyone like a book?"

"Only my kids and you. What's up, Harry?"

Harry sat back down at the kitchen table and crossed his legs comfortably. "I don't know. Call it old instincts. I know writers, Molly. I worked with them all my life. Studied them, wrote about them, idolized them. I never knew a writer who was not obsessed with working, especially a guy like Roland Heinz, who had to stay three steps ahead of his demons. If you read both of those books very carefully, and believe me, I have; you get a strong feeling that Garnet Granger was missing a morph or two. I could be wrong..."

"I don't see it, but I have not studied Roland." Then Molly thought of something almost too obvious. "For Christ sake, Harry, why don't you ask him? Tomorrow might be too late."

Harry's right eyebrow rose just slightly. "You're right, of course, but I mean...can I?"

"I told him I'd come back this evening. They'll let you in with me. Roland gave me his power of attorney."

"Really?"

Molly nodded. "She was enjoying this little revelation. Something about the word 'power,' she thought. She grabbed her car keys off the table and gave her head a 'let's go' jerk. Harry smiled and went to get his coat. The cake the girls had baked was sitting in a Tupperware cake holder on the counter and she grabbed that, too, although she doubted Roland could eat it. There was a note scotch taped to with both girls' writing. That he would devour. A minute later they were off to St. Agnes Hospital and Roland Heinz.

"Harry, I never met anyone who tried so damned hard to be my friend," Roland whispered. He had just put aside the note from the girls, which he had read twice, smiling broadly. The nurse's station got the cake.

Molly had been surprised to find that Roland had been moved out of ICU to a room during the time she had gone home. The basic monitor's were still hooked up, but the drama and dread of ICU was removed and Roland seemed cheerful, if still very weak.

"You were always a tough nut to crack, Mr. Heinz. I truly wish we could have spent more time together over the years," said Harry. Molly was touched that they were holding hands.

"I always wanted to apologize to you," said Roland.

"For what?"

"Shit, Harry, for never making you any money."

"Yeah, well, that was my own fault. Who knew, for god's sake what was locked up inside of you?" Harry smiled and gave Roland's hand an extra squeeze. "But, I accept your apology, you old son of a bitch. Bob Becker reminds me every time I see him at some book publisher's convention that I dropped you into his lap."

"Well, you know how it went back then," said Roland. "He dangled the cash and I followed it into his web."

Harry saw his opening. It was now or never, he figured. "Maybe it's not too late, Roland. You got anything laying around that farmhouse? Any notes, diaries? Hell fire, is there any doodling I can use? You went unpublished too long."

"Hah, everyone asks me that question. Maybe I just dried up for a few years. It happens. Writer's block and all that."

"Bullshit."

Roland faked insulted outrage. "Listen, friend, if there was anything, and I'm not saying there is, it would all be published posthumously. If I don't make a dime, neither do you."

"I still say bullshit."

"I'm dying and all you can say is bullshit?"

"More bullshit, Roland. I read your books. You don't believe in death."

Roland put his index finger to his lips and looked to where Molly was sitting trying not to pay attention to them. "Let's just say as the hour approaches my respect for the reaper grows deeper. Anyway, it ain't death; it's dying that sucks, Harry. What ever you do, don't let them take you to the hospital."

Harry knew that Roland had artfully deflected him and he let the idea of unpublished material drop. He had taken his shot and missed. Having scratched that itch he was free to enjoy his visit. While Molly went to the gift shop and browsed, the two bookmen recovered a lot of old ground. After a while, Roland got tired and had to beg off. Molly returned just in time to kiss Roland good night and then she and Harry drove back to Ghost Farm. They were both relieved to have found Roland doing so well. They also were both very hungry and talked about food possibilities.

A phone call found Mike, Carrie and the girls back at the farm and there was a casserole in the oven and wine had been opened. It was too late to go out on a Sunday night anyway. Molly saw that almost every light in the house was on as they drove up to it. It looked like a picture postcard of a warm house on a cold night. She mentioned it to Harry, but saw that he had dozed off, chin on chest. It had been another long day.

CHAPTER TWENTY-FOUR

I went deer hunting for the first and last time when I was about twelve. A friend from school and his father invited me to go Up North with them to a family hunting cabin. I was very excited to go along since my dad was passed and I had no relatives nearby who hunted. The romance of the gun is strong in a young boy and I remember the friend's dad showing me how to use the rifle that they loaned me for the trip. It was a bolt action gun from Montgomery Ward and nothing too fancy. Didn't matter, I held it like it was a piece of the true cross. I remember walking in the rain along a forest road three abreast looking for deer, feeling like a man. I had no idea what I would do if one crossed my sights, but I knew I would figure something out. I was looking down at the gun in my hands when the shooting started. A couple deer had crossed the road and stopped, no doubt surprised to see us. The father dropped one and the son missed his. I fumbled with my gun and never got off a shot. When we walked up to the deer that was shot it was still alive and struggling, kicking its feet and making terrible noises, like a mad goose. Blood was spraying from its nostrils. The father put his gun to the deer's head and told us he was going to put it out of its misery. I learned the truest meaning of irony that day, though I didn't know it until much later in my life.

After the late supper, Mike and Carrie left and Harry and the girls headed up to bed. Mel and Sony had met Harry many times and were always happy and excited to see him. Having him stay with them in the house in this faraway land of Wisconsin made them think something was up, but they didn't know yet if it was good or bad that he was there. When Molly put them to be she had to answer their questions.

"Mr. Stompe came because he is an old friend of Papa's," Molly explained as she tucked the girls into her bed.

"Is Papa going to come home soon?" asked Sonia. She, in her innocence, always cut right to the chase.

Molly saw in Melanie's eyes that she wanted this answer, too. Molly never lied to the girls for any reason, but she was tempted to now before they went to sleep. She wrestled with herself for a second or two.

"Papa is sick and might not come home." She let it sink in. "You both have had experience with people you know and love leaving you, though you sometimes don't remember. Papa is..."

"Papa is dying, isn't he?" Melanie interrupted.

"Is he, Mom?" said Sonia.

"Okay, listen, his heart is old and tired and yes, he may not live much longer. I want you to say a prayer for Papa and then go to sleep. He loves you both very much and that is what he wants you to do."

Prayer was as far as her religious training of the girls had gone. Since they had both been born to other cultures and faiths, she had decided to let them sort it out when they were old enough to decide for themselves how they wanted to find God. Their bedtime prayer was more of a peaceful blessing than anything else. A thank you for the day. Molly watched it happen as the girls turned away from each other in the bed and closed their eyes. She had told them that the hand-folding was like dialing God's phone number. The prayers were always silent with sleep coming close behind.

Molly remembered to grab her tape recorder and then went to the bedroom door and stood with her hand on the light switch. She thought for a moment that it wasn't fair for Roland to bring them here when he knew he was going to die. But, then she realized what a blessing this had been for the girls to connect to him so totally. A blessing for all of them. A lifetime with their Papa could not have been fuller than this week. She turned off the light, but kept the door slightly open to the hall.

Harry's bedroom door was closed, but Molly could hear snoring coming rhythmically from within. The red wine at dinner had finished off Harry's day, she thought. Now she planned to finish off hers out in the writing studio with the sound of Roland's voice. She wanted to hear it more person-ally than professionally tonight. When she settled onto the studio couch and pulled a blanket over her, she switched on the recorder. It was in the middle of a part of the interview, but she didn't care. In the darkened room it was like having Roland sitting next to her.

Hell is an interesting place in one respect, Molly. You see, only the living can go there and too many of us make the trip. In the depths of my depression I would lay in a sort of deep trance, not sleeping, but not quite awake either. I felt the very real sensation of being deep underground. That part the the-ologians got right. Hell is definitely 'down' in the direction of the human mind. In my case, it was like the cellar of an old and empty house. Once you are down there, the first instinct is to explore. I found that this place was damp, but not really cold or hot. There were no windows, but a pale green light was coming in from somewhere. There were passageways leading off in various directions, but they led nowhere. There were no doors or exits of any kind.

Being in this place was painless at first. I thought, okay, this isn't any worse than my life up above. If this is where I am supposed to be I'll make the best of it. This is where the true nature of the place kicked in. There was no best of it. It doesn't take long to realize that without the sky, the sun, the stars, the clouds, the birds; that you are out of the sight of God. If God is love, then Hell is being unloved. I felt despair of the most profound kind. Not even death could get you out of this place. I don't know how I am even finding the words to explain it to you, dear. It was the worst place imaginable. But, then that was the key, wasn't it?"

If I was vividly imagining my place in hell, then couldn't I imagine my escape? Again, if God, the Creator had already been in my brain, allowing the images and creating the ideas then there must be one unused flash of electrical energy that could reverse the concept, help me to locate the cellar door. First I heard some far off barking. Sorry. Then the steps lead-ing upward. Imagination. And then I found the door. Writing. It was the size and shape of the eye of a needle. I invented the way out of hell on the day when I conceived and wrote the first lines of The Tap Root. So, you see Molly, I created Garnet Granger in my own image. The way I saw myself at the time. Life had made me too large to pass through the needle's eye. It took her and me four hundred and fifty-six pages to find our way out of hell. We uninvented the damned place. We held each other's hand all the way. She was a wonderful traveling companion.

So there you have it, Molly. The barking dog was the catalyst. To be loved again was the motive. The imagination was the way up. And the books were the way out. It is easier to understand if you read the books than have me explaining it into this damned tape recorder. Shut that thing off now.

Molly obeyed Roland's wish and turned off the recorder. She was instantly aware how cold it had gotten in the studio. The wood-burning stove was cold and she didn't have a clue how to light it. Throwing off the blanket she left the shed and headed back into the house. Above her the midnight sky was dazzling with stars.

A mile down Highway 151 Mike and Carrie were waiting for the last of the Sunday night drinkers to head home from The Back Room. Carrie had promised the girl who filled in for her earlier that she would come in by midnight and close the bar. It was now 12:30 AM and a few die hard farmers were shaking dice and acting very comfortable. Bar etiquette did not allow Carrie to shoo away any paying customers just because it was late, but these old boys were barely drinking and making a lot of noise. Mike sat in his usual spot near the door and windows and watched Carrie glower at the gamblers. She already had the bar rag tossed over her shoulder. He was wondering why he loved that pissed off look of hers so much. He waved her down.

"Don't frown like that. You're face will get stuck looking that way," Mike said as he put his hand over Carries wet fingers.

"I just want them to go home. Most nights I wouldn't care, but not tonight," Carrie sighed.

"Look at it this way, honey. We have the rest of the night and probably all day tomorrow to lie around and recharge. I can't wait to spend the whole day with you."

She looked at him and gave him a pretty smile. "Me, too, but if something happens tomorrow we may have to watch the girls again. I don't mind, but..."

"Yeah, I know. Roland."

"Molly said it is touch and go. She said his doctor said it was a matter of days."

"I would sure like to see him sometime tomorrow."

"Me, too. We'll work it out with Molly, okay?"

Mike suddenly felt the barrier of the bar between them and didn't want it there. He could feel her gravity turned on high and drawing him to her. It was a very strong pull right then. He took her wrist and gently pulled her closer as he leaned up and over the bar. They kissed and drew loud hoots from the boys with the dice cup. Carrie broke the kiss and turned to them.

"Can't you old farts take a hint? Go home and get some of your own."

More cat calls and whistles arose, but the statement seemed to have broken the spell of the dice and first one farmer said it was late and then another. They were finally bundling up and heading out. Carrie walked down and turned off the overhead TV at the other end of the bar and suddenly the silence was deafening. She came around to the other side of the bar and walked intentionally sexy up to Mike.

"We're alone, Michael. What are you gonna do about it?"

Mike looked around and then out the window. "In here?"

Carrie shrugged. "You ever do it in a bar?"

"No. Have you?"

"Not that I can remember." Carrie then went to the door and locked it from the inside. She hit the house light switch by the door and suddenly The Back Room became a very different place. At that moment they both knew that the week of books, and babysitting, and casseroles, and holding hands in the moonlight was requiring a little something extra. But, just when Mike was about to pounce on his willing prey, there was a loud tap on the window. Someone was out there.

"We're closed!" Carrie yelled at the top of her lungs, but now there was a banging on the door.

"Shit," Carrie said as she went to unlock the door. "Somebody forgot something."

When she opened the door, Meg Bollander was standing there with a foolish smile.

"I saw the lights just go out when I pulled up," Meg said. "Thought maybe I could get a night cap."

"Well..." said Carrie drawing out the word into its intended meaning which was 'no.'

"Carrie, its okay," said Mike. "One more drink won't hurt." He recognized a spell when it was broken. Carrie let Meg in and introduced him to Mike.

"Mike this is Mrs. Bollander. She lives in the place behind Roland's."

"Oh, well, any friend of Roland..." Mike began.

Meg took a stool and started to shoot a dagger eye at Mike, but caught herself. She didn't want a confrontation with these young people. Especially since she knew she had just broken in on something that was going to get hot and heavy. She remembered hot and heavy so she spoke softly.

"Mr. Heinz and I are not exactly friends, but he used to be my brother-in-law. I actually came down here to ask this young lady if she knew anything about how he is doing. I saw the ambulance again last night."

Carrie had picked up bits and pieces from Molly about Meg's relationship with Roland and knew better than to judge or probe. Simple information was the best thing.

"He's back in the hospital, Mrs. Bollander, and he's not doing too well. His doc says a matter of days. What do you want to drink?" Carrie moved back behind the bar after turning the lights back on.

"Oh, just give me a shot of blackberry, dear. It goes good with the snow."

Five minutes later Meg was gone with her information and Mike and Carrie decided to head across the street to her warm and waiting bed. Making love on a bar is one of those things that only happens when the planets are all aligned perfectly and no one raps on the window.

Back at Ghost Farm it was 4:44 AM when the house phone hanging on the kitchen wall rang its loud and foreign sounding ring.

CHAPTER TWENTY-FIVE

Once on one of my trips to Chicago to visit my book people, I got to see my first stage play, the name of which is not important. Such an experience in my neck of the woods is only available on the amateur level. This play was astounding to me. Though I had written a couple novels by this time, I had never even considered what it would be like writing for the stage...or movies for that matter. As I watched the play my head was spinning, trying to figure out how the writer pulled it off but, soon a couple things became apparent. The first was how the story was advanced by using only dialogue and stage craft. The actors on the stage could be the characters in my books, but they, with the director's help, were bringing mere words to life. What I would write as background description was employed in set design and lighting. I thought about this for hours after the play concluded. How could I use what I had learned and enjoyed in that theater in my own style of writing? For the first time I began to see my characters as actors on the stage of my page. I began to allow them to do things in my head that I would not normally think they should do. I began to move them in their situations from mark to mark, allowing them to dance through my chapters. I never tried to write a play, but I folded the technique into my novels. It allowed me to write in three dimensions; and then later in four.

Molly Costello stood in her robe, holding the kitchen phone to her ear, listening to a voice explain to her what had just happened at the hospital. As she listened, the other bath robed house guests at Roland Heinz's Ghost Farm wandered into the kitchen. Melanie and Sonia went silently to the kitchen table and slumped into chairs, watching and waiting with sleepy eyes. Harry Stompe was more alert and instinctively began to fumble with the automatic coffee maker, drawing water from the sink into the pot. Molly's conversation consisted of a couple 'I see's' a couple 'thank you's' and one resolute 'goodbye.'

Everyone in the kitchen knew the gist of the call. After all, it was nearly 5AM, early, dark, and foreboding. Molly, at first, could only nod her head to the questioning eyes. Then addressing the girls first, she told them Papa was gone. The children looked stunned but seemed to understand. They said nothing. Harry, however, wanted some details.

"What happened, Mol, he was doing so well last night?"

"The night nurse said he went into cardiac arrest and died in his sleep."

Melanie then spoke up. "That means it didn't hurt, right Mom?"

"Yes, dear. Papa went very peacefully. He just went to sleep."

"He went to Heaven, huh, Mom?" said Sony.

Molly went over to the table and put both arms around the girls. "He absolutely went to Heaven today, babes." She was fighting tears that might alarm the girls. Harry saw it and jumped in.

"Hey, you two, let's go back up to bed and we can talk about this later. I'll go with you, okay?'

"Mom?" Melanie was looking for permission to go back to bed. Sonia was already walking away.

"Go with Harry, girls, he'll tuck you in and talk to you." She turned to Harry. "Thanks, boss."

Harry gave a weak, but warm smile and led the girls back upstairs. Molly finished the coffee pot prep and then sat down at the table. As she waited for the coffee to drip, her tears began to pour. They were the kind of tears shed at the end of a sad, but lovely old movie. It was a heartbreak that she knew was coming, but human emotions don't know about nuance when they are triggered. The hard fact was that Roland would not be coming home. The dream week was ending in sadness. Her article would be a farewell. Her life would be forever altered by his. This thought brought on the recovery sniffle, the loud one that makes one shake their head to clear it. Roland Heinz had indeed changed her life, but it was all for the better. The tear glands shut down and allowed her to call Mike's cell phone. She had promised she would call no matter how late or early if she had any news.

Mike and Carrie's phone call found them tangled up in each other and the bedding in the wake of a serious session of making new, strong love. Mike's cell phone was somewhere in the room, but not quite within easy reach so he had to locate it and call Molly back. He made the call with Carrie's ear next to his on a warm pillow.

"Molly, what's going on?"

"Sorry to wake you up. He's gone, Mike. Cardiac arrest. Just a little while ago."

Mike felt Carrie squeeze his free hand. She had heard the message clearly.

"Um, Jesus, Molly, that was so fast. I mean, he was fine earlier, right?"

"I don't think he was fine all week, but he was hanging on for us."

"Had that feeling, too, actually." Mike's voice was beginning to choke up. "So, what's next? What can we do? Me and Carrie."

"Go back to sleep if you can. I have to call Roland's lawyer and find out what I am supposed to do from here. I am sure there are instructions. I may need help with the girls later. Harry is taking care of them now."

"How are they doing?"

"Well, pretty good. I already knew my girls were brave. The thing is they adopted Roland so fast, I think there will be a delayed reaction to losing him so quickly. I mean, it's like here he is and there he goes. I should have considered more what I was bringing them into when they came here. And yet..." The thought dangled.

"What, Molly?"

"And yet, this was all so good for them on so many levels." Then Molly's voice changed timbre and tone. "Let's sort it out later. Why don't you come over, say around nine for breakfast and we will all sit down together. I should have some details by then."

The conversation ended with that agreement. Mike and Carrie cuddled and talked about Roland for the next hour and Molly dialed up Patrick Zeneb, attorney at law. Her call found him in his car.

"Patrick here," he answered.

"Mr. Zaneb, its Molly Costello."

"Ms. Costello, I was just about to call you. I just left the hospital. Let me say, I am so sorry. You must know I loved Roland like a brother." It was difficult to not use profanity in a sentence for Zeneb, even under these circumstances, but he made the conscious effort. His pain came across without the emphasis of habitual cursing.

"We all loved him," said Molly. Her mind immediately flew to Meg Bollander, who would be her next call. "What do I do next from here?"

"Okay, listen, Molly, I am due in court early this morning so I am tied up until about noon. Can you come in to my office then? There are lots and lots of details for you to go over as the executor of his will."

"Is that the same as power of attorney?"

"Almost, but slightly different now that he has passed," Patrick explained.

"His will. Is there a funeral to arrange? What?" Molly's mind was suddenly overwhelmed with all the various things she now needed to consider.

"I will lay it all out for you later. Why don't you try to collect your thoughts for now and take care of your kids? I know Roland was fond of them and I am sure it was the same for them. Trust me, Molly, that he has made very sure that this will be a very easy process for you. I can tell you there will be no funeral per se. Today is Monday. Plan on a small get together at your...I mean Roland's house for say, Wednesday. That sound right?"

"I guess. But, we'll talk about everything right?"

"Absolutely. I'll see you at noon."

"Thank you. See you then."

Molly wanted to get the next call out of the way before the kids came down stairs again. To insure her privacy, she went out into Roland's studio, even thought it was freezing inside. She again pulled a blanket over her on the couch, took a deep breath, and dialed Meg's phone number. Meg was an early riser and answered right away.

"Yes?" Meg's voice already had an edge of apprehension.

"Meg, it's Molly. I'm sure you know why I called."

"Yeah, I do. Gimme a second while I fill my coffee cup." She put the phone down for about ten seconds. "What time did he die?"

"We got the call around quarter to five."

Silence.

"Meg?"

"Sorry, Molly. I knew this was coming, but the news is strange now that I am hearing it."

"You had a strange relationship with that man."

More silence.

"Look, Meg, I figured you would want me to call you," Molly said softly. She was picturing the face of the woman on the other end of the phone. "You want me to get off the phone?"

Molly heard Meg's throat clearing. "Well, yes, thank you for the information, dear. I am sorry, but this has somehow thrown me this morning. I need to go."

"Meg, there is going to be a gathering here on Wednesday. Will you come?"

"Um, Wednesday? I don't know. I mean I don't think so."

Molly was suddenly exasperated. "Okay, get back to me. I have to go now, too."

They hung up in unison and both wondered what the other was thinking for the rest of the morning.

When Mike and Carrie arrived, the girls flew to them. Somehow Melanie and Sonia were able to release their version of grief to their newest friends easier than to their mother. Molly was not hurt at all and was more than grateful that the girls were able to talk to someone about their Papa dying. Molly brought coffee to the living room where Mike had Sonia leaning on him and Carrie had Melanie. She acted the part of a waitress, serving silently, but with a smile. This part of the process was somehow working and she wouldn't break the spell with words. The girls were crying and Mike and Carrie were hugging. The emotions were slowly being bled off. It was the first step of healing.

It was another cold and clear morning, the sun not quite up over The Ledge and Harry suggested a short walk. Molly thought it was a good idea. He had not seen the farm in the daylight and it would not only be diverting, but a good chance to talk and escape for a few minutes.

"That's his studio," Molly said as they headed out. She knew Harry wanted to see the inside, but she wasn't ready to let him in there yet. She kept walking and led him through the barnyard past the yellow barn.

"There's an owl in there."

"Huh?"

"Oh, I'll explain later. Harry, I have a million things going through my mind."

"That's why we're walking, Mol."

She leaned into Harry and gave him a nudge with her shoulder. She had always needed Harry on one level or another.

"You talk to Pat Zeneb yet?" Harry asked. Great white blasts of vapor spewed from his mouth as he talked.

"You know him?"

"I've dealt with him a few times. Good man. He's been Roland's friend and lawyer forever."

Molly realized that they had been talking about Roland in the present tense. It was a subtle and difficult adjustment to assign him to the past. "We spoke earlier."

"What are the arrangements to be?"

"I'm going to meet with him at his office around noon to lay it all out. I, of course, want you in on all this."

"Okay," Harry said, nodding emphatically.

"I have to ask you, Harry, I only knew Roland for about a week and you knew him for a long time. Why am I handling all the legal stuff?"

"Because that's the way Roland wanted it."

"But why? I don't get it." She stopped walking and turned to Harry. The sun was now sending long shadows down from The Ledge across the snowy field.

"I'm sure Pat Zeneb will have details."

"But, you know something about all this, right?"

The sunlight was now on Harry's face like a bare light bulb in an interrogator's room. Dodging the question was maybe possible, but he felt the time was right.

"I know some things," he said. "Good things."

"What are you saying, Harry?"

"Let me put it this way, Molly. Roland chose you to be more than just his interviewer."

"Go on."

"He researched you pretty completely and contacted me a couple weeks before that request letter was written."

"He researched me? Why?"

"He saw something in your writing, he said. He ended up reading everything you had ever written. He then went deeper and found articles about you and the girls. Your lives."

Molly's mind went back to the clipping Roland showed her of the article about her after the adoptions. Things were falling into place.

"It's rather hard to explain, but told me he wanted to tell his story to not only you, but to you as family. Molly I think he had already adopted you and the girls before he met you. Do you understand any of that?"

Molly shoved her hands into her jacket pockets and started walking again. She was thinking and filling in the gaps of the previous week. Now she saw it all very clearly.

"Yeah, no, I get it now."

"You do, huh? And...?

"And, it doesn't matter how or why this week happened." She took about a dozen more crunching steps across the crusty snow, then abruptly stopped and smiled "Life is tricky, eh Harry?"

'You're okay with all this?"

"What can I do? Roland wrote out this week like it was his last chapter of his last book. He turned his fictitious characters into real life people. Harry, he knew I would get it. My God, he almost beat it into my head." She resumed walking; now a little lighter, it seemed.

"He never could separate his real life from his writing," she continued, "because in his mind there was absolutely no difference. Once he had worked out the process of changing his life and behavior there was no turning back. He started writing his own life, which I guess included me and the girls. I am probably going to spend the rest of my life figuring out all the different nuances of this, but yes, I do get it. Actually, it is quite unique. Crazy, but good crazy."

"You probably understand much more than I do. Your article should be a doozy."

"I will make it special...for him."

"Good, can we go back now, my ass is freezing."

Molly looked at Harry red face with all the steam coming off it and suddenly broke out laughing. "Wouldn't want your old ass to freeze and fall off your hips. Let's go."

"Shit, you even sound like him now."

"Good!" Molly barked as they turned and hurried back to the warm farmhouse.

CHAPTER TWENTY-SIX

*The greatest word in the language of Man is forgiveness.
Much has been written about it in concept, creed, and canon.
Some think of the term as the wiping clean of a debt on the
soul. But, really to forgive something requires two mutual acts
performed simultaneously. The forgiven must forgive the for-
giver for forgiving them. Ouch. It makes the brain hurt to think
about it this way, but it is essential. To forgive is raise yourself
above another person. To be forgiven is to bow. But, who was
ever on their knees looking up at someone that did not curse
them for their height? True forgiveness is done on even and
common ground. It requires only a will and a single prop: a
mirror. Therefore, I have always found forgiveness to be best
bestowed in a bathroom...while shaving at the break of a new
day.*

The sun was blazing into the sparse and spare law office
of Patrick Zeneb as Molly and Harry sat waiting for Pat to
arrive. His secretary had provided some tepid and bitter coffee, which Harry supposed had been left over from early
morning. They both took a sip and set the foam cups aside
just as Pat burst into the room.

"So sorry I'm late, Ms. Costello...oh, for the love of God is
that Harry Stompe?" Pat rushed past Molly and almost rang
the handshake off of Harry. They were still shaking hands as
he turned and spoke over his shoulder to Molly.

"Haven't seen this yard bird in years."

"Long time, Patrick," said Harry as he freed his hand and
nodded to Molly. Pat caught the cue.

"Oh God, forgive me my manners. My condolences to
you...to both of you. It's a sad day."

"Yes, it is," said Molly, "but both of you knew Roland
much longer than I did. Let me return the sentiment right back
to you, Mr. Zeneb."

"Yes, yes, thank you...say, can I call you Molly? Please
call me Pat. This business we have to do would be better

served if it is done informally. I know Roland would want it that way. Everyone agree?"

Molly smiled. "Of course. Call me Molly for the love of God!"

Pat was stunned for a moment, looking at Molly and then at Harry. "You old son of a bitch, Harry! Telling tales about me, eh?"

"Actually, it was Roland," Molly giggled. "He did a pretty good impression of you. Pat, I felt like I knew you before I walked in here. By all means, let's be friends for Roland."

Pat chuckled deeply and then settled in to the business of the day. He produced a folder from a drawer in his stark Amish desk and began to rifle through it. He organized some papers into three piles and then looked up at Molly, who had been watching him carefully. She was wondering what was coming next.

"Molly, heck, we can go all through this legal stuff point by point or I can just give you the condensed version."

"You can give me the short version, Pat. My mind is not in the mood for legalese today."

"Figured. Okay, here it is in a nutshell...a quite extraordinary nutshell, I must say. Roland Heinz knew he was dying for quite a while so he made very precise decisions as to how he was to be handled and where the burial was to be, etc. He will be cremated today at Stanhope and his ashes are to be placed in a wooden box that he designed himself. You will see it later.

"He also made some very recent changes to his will. In fact he did some of it only last week. The summation of that will is that you, Molly Costello, are sole heir to the Roland Heinz estate pending one detail that you will have to agree to."

Molly was in shock. Harry was amused.

"Wha...what detail?" Molly whispered.

"You must agree to a posthumous adoption. He wanted you to become his daughter, Molly.

While Molly gasped Harry asked an obvious question. "Is that legal?"

"Couldn't find any loopholes. Roland already signed his declaration. It only requires your signature, Molly, and then I have arranged to expedite it through a judge that owes me a bunch of favors." He winked. "Once the decree is filed, you would immediately become his legal daughter and heiress. And Molly, the estate is considerable."

Molly had to consciously make an effort to close her gaping mouth. Things were sinking in very slowly. Harry reached over and put his arm around her and gave her a strong squeeze.

"By the end of the week," Pat continued, "You will own the farm and everything on it and in it. You will own the accumulating royalties from his books. You will be given the control of his bank accounts and assume the responsibilities of his debts. By the way, he doesn't owe a dime to anyone, but me, of course. We can settle that later. Questions at this point?"

Molly could only shake her head slowly, but gradually found her voice. "Is this real? I mean I only met Roland a week ago."

"Remember our conversation this morning, Molly," Harry inserted. "This is all very real, isn't it Patrick?"

"As God is my witness, it's all right as rain. You wanna sign this so my secretary can take it over to the courthouse right now?" Pat slid a paper toward Molly and pointed to the signature line. He then handed her a pen.

"Does this mean the girls are going to be his grandchildren, too?"

"Well, yes it does. In fact he even set up a trust fund for them already, whether or not you sign this. Read it."

Molly scanned the paper catching the gist of it. It was all just as Pat said. She looked up and searched Pat's eyes and then Harry's. They were both beaming. She took the pen and with it became Roland's daughter, the owner of Ghost Farm and the legacy of Roland Heinz. Pat buzzed his secretary and sent her off to the courthouse with the packet. He knew the wheel had already been greased and that the deal would be done before the ink was dry. They all shook hands and then hugs as Molly and Harry left to go home. Pat would be at the house on Wednesday for the gathering. He was bringing Roland.

The next twenty-four hours were passed quietly. People caught up on their sleep. Mike and Carrie had taken charge of the girls for most of the day and kept them overnight at Carrie's on Monday night. On Tuesday everyone had pitched in to prepare for the reception the next day. With Patrick's help, Molly had been able to assemble the names of a few people who had been invited to come. Of course, the Dorfman's were the only relatives, but Roland had some old friends and neighbors that jumped at the chance to come by and pay their respects. Few people, including the Dorfman's had ever been inside Ghost Farm and were curious about the place.

Molly had also worked with Patrick and Harry on writing the obituary for not only the local newspaper, but also for wire services that would send the news of Roland's passing to the whole world:

Obituary

Roland Cobb Heinz
January 29, 1939–January 26, 2009

Roland Heinz, noted author and twice winner of the Pulitzer Prize for Literature passed away Sunday at St. Agnes Hospital in Fond du Lac, Wisconsin. Roland was preceded in death by his father, William Roland Heinz, his mother, Betty Hallstom Heinz, both of Fond du Lac; and his best friend, Sorry Heinz. Roland, a resident of Pipe, Wisconsin, is survived by his daughter, MollyCostello, of Pipe, Wisconsin, and her two daughters, Melanie Mai Costello and Sonia Farah Costello. Private services will be held at the Heinz-Costello farm in Pipe on Wednesday, January 28th. Memorial contributions may to be given to The Fond du Lac Public Library Fund in his name.

Everyone agreed that Roland would have appreciated the brevity of the obit and also the recent changes pertaining to his surviving family. Molly also thought it would give some of the locals a nice piece of gossip to chew on. Meg came foremost in her mind along those lines. She wondered what to do about Meg Bollander. Perhaps she would make one more attempt to get her to stop by the next day.

When the obituary ran in the local paper on Tuesday evening, Molly got the web version of it on her computer. She found it very interesting that besides the obituary, there was only a short story devoted to the town's world famous author. Beneath the story was a space for reader's comments and the few that were added posted comments like, 'I didn't even know he was from here' and 'never heard of the guy.' Of course, Roland knew before he died that his legacy as a great writer had never been recognized locally. Part of that was his own fault for never promoting himself or his books. Local book people knew he was around there somewhere, but never sought him out. Respected privacy was a Wisconsin trait for the most part. He had always been fine with that.

Meg Bollander still got the evening paper delivered to her mailbox and went out to get it as soon as she saw the old station wagon of the delivery woman pull away. She sat at her kitchen table and scanned the front page and then tore through to the obituaries. She let her finger follow the lines as she read them. She read the item three times. She was not only dumb stuck by the part about Molly being his adopted daughter, but something else caught her eye.

"Who the fuck is Sorry Heinz?" she wondered out loud.

She reached for her phone to call Molly, but then reconsidered it. She made herself a Kessler's and water instead and went into the living room to sit among her collectibles and sort out her thoughts. Part of her wanted to go to the service the next day, but the other part, the part that steered her life for all these years told her to stay home and drink the next two days away. Of course, it would be much easier to do the latter. Goddamn you Roland Heinz, she thought, as she picked up her copy of *A Winter Light* and opened it to a random page. She read and sipped whiskey until she fell asleep. On this night she followed Garnet Granger deep into a dream within a dream.

CHAPTER TWENTY-SEVEN

There used to be an orchard on the north side of my farm house. I am guessing apples although there is nothing remaining of the trees except for several neat rows of stumps. I never had a clue as to why those trees were removed, but what was left was a plush green field of purple clover in the late Spring. Up until a few years ago this was an amazing attraction for honey bees. The field was so full of worker bees gathering nectar that I could hear the hum from inside my kitchen. I used to take a chair out to the edge of the field and watch their tireless labor and just wonder at the industry. I found some broken hive boxes at the far end of the old orchard so I knew the previous owners had collected the honey. I pictured Ball Jars filled with liquid gold at the end of each summer. Of course, a few years ago the bees disappeared without a trace. Some said it was global warming or climate change, but explanatory theories are not important to me. I miss the hum. Once while watching them I wondered if I would trade the long life of a human for the short life of a flying honey bee. If I had gotten my wish, I would be long dead.

To the delight of Molly, the folks who had been invited to Roland's memorial gathering arrived on time and laden with food. Pat Zaneb told her they would. It was a Wisconsin tradition and now one entire table in the living room was filled with Nesco-Roasters and dishes-to-pass. Pat told her, only half joking, that the Nesco-Roaster should have been included on The Great Seal of the State of Wisconsin. The meals, which included scalloped potatoes and ham, roasted chicken with dressing, hamburger patties in gravy, spare ribs with sauerkraut, and a dozen variations of sausage filled the house with an intoxicating variety of aromas. The desserts were piled on every available surface in the house. And no one was shy about eating or drinking.

The girls had gone shopping the day before with Carrie and were wearing new dresses. Both of them still clung to

Mike and Carrie, following them around the house like puppies. Molly had not had a chance to sit them down and explain the changes that were taking place in all their lives. There would be plenty of time for that later after the guests had gone.

The Dorfman's had been the first to arrive with Mort setting up his own grill outside the kitchen to fry some brats. He stayed out there in the cold, beer in hand, for most of the day. Barb brought in the first Nesco as her experience told her it was best to be early and find an open electrical outlet. Fuses could blow. When she got her arms free she hugged Molly and the girls as though they had been family forever.

"Oh, my goodness," said Barb Dorfman with little grunts to emphasize the hugs. "Don't you girls look sweet? And Molly, Molly, welcome to the family. I read the thing in the paper and cried for joy." Molly noted the girls seemed oblivious to the comment.

"Thank you, Barb. I'm still not used to it."

"Well, there aren't too many of us around so Mort and I were so happy to hear the news." Barb then spotted the wooden box on a table by the picture window. There were no flowers, but the two great books rested beside the shiny box. "Is that Roland?"

"Yes, it is," answered Molly. It seemed so strange to have to introduce the box as Roland. It almost made her start to cry, but she caught herself. Today was not about tears. She had noticed Sonia's fascination for the box as well as Melanie's aversion to it. The box itself was simple varnished pine, but it had the Ghost Farm cornflower print on the top and she wondered who had done it and how. It was perfect for Roland; she mused and then became aware that Barb was still talking.

"'Course, we never read any of his books. We're just not readers, me and Mort," Barb noted as she put her hand on the box gently. "But, he was such a good writer,"

Other people showed up and introduced themselves to Molly. She met Pat's wife, Sally, whom she liked immediately because she got into the kitchen and began helping out with the dishes and cups. Pat set up the bar on the kitchen counter and made sure everyone had a full drink all afternoon. Molly smiled as he made Old Fashions and handed them off with his own epitaph for his old friend and client.

"Roland Heinz was the goddamned best friend I ever had."

A couple of old farmers came by with their wives and introduced themselves as neighbors, who had done the remodeling of the Ghost Farm. Molly thanked them and made sure everyone got food and drink. One little old lady, that no one had introduced to her, was having no trouble finding refills for her Old Fashions as she was needing one about every three to four minutes. Molly was curious and made her way over.

"Hello, I don't think we have met. I'm Molly Costello." Molly held her hand out and the old woman took it into her own cold, wet hand.

"Yeah, I know who you are. I'm old lady Dankermann, the village crone."

Molly was at first speechless thinking she had a party crasher on her hands, but after a long moment the woman burst into a deep cackle.

"That line always throws 'em. Never mind my humor, dear. I was Rollie's neighbor and Catechism teacher many, many years ago. I used to live here in Pipe when his folks were still alive."

"So you go way back?" said Molly.

"Back to the goddamn Stone Age," said Mrs. Dankermann, with a wink. "I just came by for a drink and to pay my respects. I tried to read one of those books once," she said, nodding towards the table with Roland's box, "but, I didn't get it. Too flowery for me. But, Rollie was a good drinker there for a while. He and I had some great discussions at the pub over in Johnsburg. He'll be missed."

"Thank you for coming, Mrs. Dankermann," said Molly. "If you need another drink, see the man over there."

"Hah, Patrick Zeneb. First time that lawyer ever served up anything, but lies...." Mrs. Dankermann walked away from

Molly muttering, but headed straight for another dose of lies and brandy.

As the afternoon wore on and before most of the people could leave, Pat tapped a spoon on a glass and signaled that he wanted to speak. The group of semi-inebriated and well fed mourners turned their attention to the lawyer as he stood by Roland's remains. Molly joined him by the table.

"Friends, may I have your attention for just a few moments?" When the hum subsided he began. "Roland gave me explicit instructions that I was not to make any speeches."

Somebody muttered, "Good."

"Yes, well, I promised so I won't. What I do want to do is make a couple announcements. As most of you know by now, Roland Heinz adopted Molly Costello and left his estate to her. The house we are standing in is now Molly's house. I would ask that none of you badger Molly for explanations, but rather accept her simply as Roland's daughter."

Someone started to applaud, but it died quickly.

"I have been instructed by Roland that this box..." Pat patted it gently, "is to be buried next to Roland's friend, Sorry out back by the lilac bushes behind the cheese shed. For those of you who don't know who Sorry was, well, it was Roland's dog."

This caused a bit of a stir, but Molly realized that everyone was nodding and smiling. Apparently these folks understood that people could be buried with their dogs if they wanted to be.

Pat continued. "Roland was, to say the least, eccentric, with his own rules and ideas about how things worked for him. As far as I every knew, he never gave a whit about wealth or status, but cared very deeply about his writing and his books. He cared about how they related to the readers who could decipher them and mine their meaning. These two books resting here next to Roland's ashes are the living testaments to all writers, all readers, and all lovers of books. It is in this spirit that I ask Mike Gabler to step forward here."

Mike, who was standing in the back, was shocked to hear his name called. He slowly walked forward with a questioning look on his face. What did he have to do with Roland's writing, he wondered? Pat Zeneb took Mike's arm and pulled him close so he could whisper in his ear. Mike listened and then pulled back as if surprised by what he had heard. Mike immediately walked to the stairway leading to the upstairs and went up. The silent group could hear his footsteps causing loud creaks in the ceiling overhead. A moment later, Mike came down the steps with an old fashioned ladies' hat box in his hands. He brought it up to where Pat stood.

"I had almost forgotten that Roland told me about this box," said Mike. "He told me to give it to Molly after he died. Thank you for reminding me, Mr. Zeneb, although I should have remembered it on my own. Molly, this is for you."

Molly was wondering, like everyone else, what Roland could possibly have left for her in a hat box. The moment of suspense, courtesy of Roland was just what the party needed. When Mike handed her the box she realized it was heavy. Very heavy. She set it down on the table next to Roland and lifted the lid.

The entire group seemed to lean in, trying to get a peek at the contents. Molly lifted an envelope out of the hat box and read the name written on it. "Actually, this is for you, Harry."

Harry Stompe had been leaning on the banister, feeling like a mere spectator among so many locals. He had a couple of drinks and was relaxed almost to the point of drowsiness when Molly called his name. He shook his head in wonder as he approached her and took the envelope. He slid his finger under the flap and took out a single sheet of lined, yellow legal pad paper. He read it silently and then stared at the hat box. He remained speechless for several long moments until someone said, 'what's it say?'

Harry looked dumbfounded by cleared his throat. "It says...well...oh hell, Molly, read this for me." He handed the note to Molly. She read it and smiled, then a tear appeared on her cheek. Harry was already reaching for his handkerchief. The gathering was silent.

"It says," Molly began. "It says, 'Harry, I think this is what you have been looking for. Please accept the contents of this box as payment for you getting me started as a writer all those years ago. You will find within my manuscript entitled *The Needle's Eye*. It now belongs to you and I am sure you will know what to do with it. As a receipt for this work, I expect you to continue to take care of and love Molly, Melanie, and Sonia as you always have. See you on the other side. Roland"

Harry could only look at Molly and just breathe. They both knew what this manuscript meant, not only to him, but to the literary world. It was like finding the Holy Grail in a hat box in Pipe, Wisconsin: unlikely, yet miraculous.

From that moment the party began to break up. Folks came by and gave Roland's box a farewell pat and then stared at the hat box filled to the top with typed pages. Harry would not move from his place near the manuscript. He alone knew its total value and could not let it out of his sight. When the guests were mostly gone, Molly had a brief conversation with Patrick Zeneb. They made arrangements to tie up the last loose ends of the estate. Pat then left with his wife. Mike and Carrie were sitting on the couch with the girls.

"You two can go if you want. The girls and I can clean this place up. In fact, I insist you spend some time together," she said to Mike and Carrie.

"You sure, Molly?" Mike asked.

"I can stay and do dishes," added Carrie.

"No, go, you guys. We are about to have a family meeting here. Just me and the girls."

"We are?" asked Melanie.

"Why?" Sonia chimed in.

Molly knew they didn't want Mike and Carrie to go, but she had to wean them off of the couple.

"Yes, ladies, we need to discuss some thing and Mike and Carrie want to spend some time alone together. And Harry, please take that hat box out to the studio. I know you are dying to start reading it. Go. Now."

Harry picked up the box and gave a little wave. He positively floated out of the house. Mike and Carrie hugged and kissed the girls and made their exit, too. Suddenly, the house was quiet.

"Let's go into the kitchen," said Molly. She wanted to get the girls away from the box of ashes that they kept stealing glances at. Molly was indeed taking control of the house. She heard it in her tone and was getting comfortable with the idea. She wondered if the girls would do the same. Seated at the kitchen table, Molly chose her words carefully. "Do you two understand what has happened?"

"Papa died," said Sonia.

"Yes, Papa died, honey. Papa died and he made us his family before he died just like I made you my family when I adopted you."

"Oh," said Sonia. Melanie was being too quiet. Molly could tell she had some deep questions.

"Mel, do you understand?"

Melanie fidgeted, rocking slowly on her seat. Her brow was knotted in thought.

"Mel? You okay?" asked Molly gently.

"Yeah, but..." said Melanie.

"But what, sweetie?"

"If Papa gave us everything, like the farm and stuff, then where are we going to live now?"

Melanie was so logical, thought Molly. Of course, this would be her concern. She had friends back in Boston. She was in a school she liked. Sonia, the same to a lesser degree.

"What do you want to do, babe?"

"I'm not sure, Mom. I mean, this place is so different from where we live..."

Molly looked at her daughters and ideas flashed before her. They could have no way of knowing what gift Roland had left them. It would be easy to sell the farm and just take what was left of the estate and go back to living the way they had before, only richer. The girls were too young to be tuned in to what Molly was feeling. She knew she could not leave this place and go back, but how could she make the girls see that Ghost Farm was much more than mere real estate. It was now their land and their home. A gift from their Papa.

"Do you want to go back home, Mel? Do you, Sonia?"

Sonia was the first to speak. "No, Mom, I want to stay here. Melanie wants to go home."

Molly should have known they had talked it over already. She should never underestimate how the kids assessed problems. "That right, Mel?"

"I don't have any friends here, Mom."

"Well, you have Carrie for one."

"Maybe she'll go back and be with Mike in Massachusetts."

Molly had not seen how far the thought process had gone with Melanie and was a little ashamed that she had not followed the threads as far as her daughter. "Okay, I see how both of you are leaning. And I understand how you feel and why. Let me think about this for a while and we will talk again tomorrow. Then Sonia got up and walked around the table to Molly's place. She put her arm around her mom.

"But, what do you want to do, Mom?

CHAPTER TWENTY-EIGHT

My prized possessions when I was a child were three old silver dollars that my grandfather had given me supposedly on my third birthday. They were kept for me by my mother in a metal lock box that all families in the day used to keep their most valuable papers and such. I think besides those coins she had immigration and citizenship papers, marriage licenses, and mortgages. Sometimes, when something would come up she would be pouring through the contents of the box. I would see her and ask to see my silver dollars from Grampa. I was allowed to hold them in my hand for a while, but I could never take them with me for fear I would lose them, or God forbid, spend them. When I was fourteen or fifteen I broke into the box and got my silver dollars out. I gave them to an older kid, who bought me and a friend a six pack of beer. Looking back it was a preview of the rest of my life. I traded my valuables for piss.

Meg Bollander had watched the coming and going of the visitors to the farm house down below her. Though she could not determine from that distance the identities of anyone, she was able to guess who most of them would be. The circle was small around The Ledge. As the day wore on she found herself obsessed with what was going on down there; what people were saying. Was anyone talking about her? She reread the obituary for the umpteenth time and still could not believe it. Of course, Meg had come to like Molly and her girls, but the time period had been so short. Only, the Devil himself, in the guise of Roland could seduce and absorb those innocents into his entanglements so quickly. It was an interesting theme, but it sounded deranged even to her. The cocktail napkin with Molly's cell phone number sat on the table. Meg's phone sat next to her chair. Meg sat next to an anxiety attack.

Mike Gabler and Carrie Stirling had taken a drive up to Stockbridge to have a late drink and talk. They both knew that

The Ledge

Mike's suitcase and camera gear was packed and sitting in Carrie's apartment and neither of them wanted to be there looking at it and what it meant. There was a supper club with a bar that was nearly empty after the dinner rush and the couple found a corner of the bar that allowed them privacy. They both ordered a draft beer and soon the bartender had departed to the other end of the bar to watch television.

"I kind of like this place," said Mike. "It's like a museum."

The supper club was decorated with too many mounted deer heads to count. Among them were an assortment of fish, fowl, and furry mammals.

"We used to come here when I was a kid," said Carrie. "I always wanted to touch the eyes of the animals and my dad would yell at me."

"How long has he been gone?"

"He died almost eleven years ago. Cancer."

"So it's just you and your mom now? I mean with your son being in California."

"Yeah, I guess. Why are you asking me all this? I mean now."

Mike looked at Carrie. He was always transfixed by those iceberg blue eyes. He thought she was so beautiful that it sometimes made him speechless. "Well, I was dancing around asking you what would happen if you moved away from here."

"Where would I be moving to?"

The eyes were distracting him. He saw a couple of silver flecks around the iris he had never noticed before. "To my house."

"To Massachusetts?"

"My house is in a town with the same name as this one."

"You live in Stockbridge? I thought you lived in Boston."

"My studio and office is in Boston. My house is in Stockbridge. It's in the Berkshire Hills. Kind of an artist colony."

"I see," said Carrie. She took a sip of her beer and swallowed it slowly, just like what she was hearing. "And what would our living arrangements be in Stockbridge. Are you proposing I move there with you to shack up?"

Now Mike noticed how feathery her dark eyebrows were. He had always loved blond hair with blue eyes with dark eyebrows. Carrie was the epitome of the look.

"Actually, I am simply proposing," he whispered.

"Like proposing or proposing proposing?" asked Carrie, her voice now a whisper, too.

"The latter, I think."

"That would be proposing proposing, correct?"

"That would be like that."

"I see."

Silence.

"What?"

"I am thinking that I have only been single for a couple days."

Silence.

"Michael?"

"What, honey?"

"Let's shack up in Stockbridge Mass for a while and then see which way the wind is blowing."

"Okay. Then you're coming with me tomorrow?"

"Yep."

"You going to quit your job?"

"Already did."

"And your mom?"

"Sisters, church, and bowling league."

"I love you."

"Me, too."

It was getting late and Molly had made sure the house was cleaned and the kids were in bed before she ventured out to the studio to check in with Harry Stompe. She brought a bottle of pretty good Merlot with her that someone had brought to the memorial party. Harry was sitting on the couch with the manuscript on the coffee table in front of him. Some pages had been turned down into a pile indicating they had been read. The greater portion of the book was waiting nearby.

"You going to stay out here all night, Harry" asked Molly as she poured him a glass of the deep red wine.

"I may be out here for a couple days."

"That good, huh?"

"Good? This is fantastic. One thousand four hundred and forty-four pages. An astounding effort."

"Now we know what he was doing for those missing years. You were right, he never stopped writing."

"Yes, and it is not just the volume. The writing is almost beyond the other two books."

"Is it the missing...what did you call it, the missing morphs of Garnet Granger?"

"Jesus, I don't know what all is in here. This is what you would call a phantasmagorical novel. I've never read anything like it. Garnet is in here, but there is so much more. It is so filthy rich with ideas, words that have never been strung together."

Harry held out his glass to Molly's. It was an invitation to a toast. "Here's to Roland," Harry said.

"To Roland," Molly answered him.

"Roland, if you are here haunting this place, then I have to say great job, my friend. Great, great job."

"What are you going to do with it?"

"I am not sure. It will have to be published, of course. The advance will be huge. But, then I also thought about previewing it, running some chapters in *Art Harvest*. We could use a boost in sales, you know?'

"That's a great idea, Harry."

"You want a peek at it, Mol.?"

"Not just yet. You enjoy it."

Harry saw that Molly was thinking about something else and now it was his turn to read her. "You're thinking about your next move, too, eh?"

"It's the girls mostly. I want to do what's right for them."

"Of course you do, Molly, but who do you think knows best what is right for your girls, you or them?"

"They get a say in it."

"Yes, but who's the adult with the intellect and gut instincts?"

"Duh, me?"

"You want to stay here don't you?"

Molly needed to hear that question put into words beyond the ones coming from inside her own head. She thought she knew the answer and wanted to test drive it.

"Yes, I want to stay. I want to live here. I have never had a sense of home like I do here. I could no more sell Ghost Farm than I could sell the girls."

"Then you stay here. I would. This place has some sort of spirit. A spirit of writing great books. It's palpable, especially in this place. This studio. Which leads me nicely into this segue. There was another note in the hat box. I found it just a little while ago. Guess it slipped down the side. Harry handed it to Molly. It was another sheet of yellow legal paper. She read it to herself.

Dear Molly,
By now you know what I did, what I planned.
In order to fulfill the last part of my will I
bequeath to you my Muse. Throw away your
damned tape recorder and let the spirit of
my cheese shed put some real writing into
your head. In other words, Molly, my dearest
daughter, Tag, You're It!!!!
Roland

Molly handed the paper to Harry and he read it quickly, handing it back to her.

"That's quite a challenge. Think you're up to it?"

Molly had her hand under her chin. She was making decisions as fast as her brain could process them. She then stood up and set down her wine glass.

"Molly?"

She smiled at Harry and he noted it was a new smile; one he had never seen before. "Yeah, I think I'm up to it," she said and made for the door.

"Where you going?"

"Gotta find that damned tape recorder. Right now!"

CHAPTER TWENTY-NINE

Garnet Granger turned and faced a pale gauzy sun, suddenly blurred by motion. A Monarch butterfly had mistaken her for a purple aster and had alighted upon her bare shoulder. The orange and black patterned wings flexed once, twice and then folded into contentment. A feeler found a pulsing place just beneath her skin and seemed to tap into her heartbeat. In that instant a mirror began to spin within her mind causing light and motion equations to fly away as shooting stars into a calm ocean of ion-rich plasma. She felt courted for the first time, courted by a single part of the whole and it made her blush. Adjusting to dizziness was her specialty, but blushing was new. It was a ruddy emotion with many fingers; some of which were touching her there...and there. She felt herself opening like a flower and she could smell her own thick perfume. She felt the butterfly's interest in her sharpen. She felt the antennae beginning to browse her skin and then she began to sense the transfer of their codes. She was being read like a book and it was her greatest ecstasy.

It was the end of March at Ghost Farm and there was the deeply organic smell of thawing soil in the air. Winter had broken its back about three weeks before and the forsythia and lilacs were beginning to bud in the farm yard. Molly Costello was walking up her driveway having just seen the girls off on the school bus into Fond du Lac. While down by the road she had also emptied the mailbox. There was a letter from Mike and Carrie to be savored later. They were still 'shacked up' in Stockbridge, Mass and obviously very happy. There was still a little snow lingering where the sun could not find it in the woods, but everything else was mostly mud or brown grass. The bulbs were coming up in front of the house, Molly noticed. Daffodils were about a week away.

It was Friday and there was plenty of time to get some projects done before fish fry at Yelanek's Supper Club. They had not missed a Friday there since Roland died and were now considered regulars by the regulars. It was like getting your citizenship papers stamped and validated. Often now, Carrie's mother, Pat had joined them and she usually brought a friend along so Molly's group of acquaintances was growing.

The girls had quickly made friends at school and two girls close to their own age lived just down the road at The Little Farmer. Their adjustment to the Midwest from the New England had been no more painful than their adjustments from Asia and Africa. Kids just did it.

Two hours earlier, just after daybreak, a work crew had entered her property on the gravel access road that led from Highway 151 to the wind turbine at the back corner of the property. She had known for weeks that they were coming, but didn't know exactly what day they would show up. She had been startled at first when Pat Zeneb had told her what was going to happen, but he assured her that it was all part of Roland's master plan and that was enough for her. Having learned this piece of information, it was nearly driving her crazy waiting to see how her neighbor would react. Well, Molly figured, Meg Bollander would soon figure it all out for herself.

Meg had been very distant since Roland had passed away. She did not return Molly's phone calls and Molly understood that she was being avoided. It was just part of living in the shadows of someone else's past. She had learned that a grudge was a grudge in Wisconsin and sometimes forgiveness was just not possible. She also knew that some people harbored grudges, but still socialized with the object of that grudge. It was complicated, but she was learning.

Meg Bollander, who didn't miss much from her perch on The Ledge, was already alert to the activity at the back of the farm that now belonged to Molly. The name of the man who had once owned it and had wronged her and her sister so long ago was deleted from her thoughts. She had watched for a couple hours as several small trucks had arrived at the wind turbine and a bunch of men had stood around it drinking coffee out of thermoses.

In a little while, two huge trucks came up the gravel road and parked side by siding. They all waited for a while and then a very big truck arrived that carried a big red crane. From that point on there was a great deal of activity. Meg watched it with great interest. First the crane was erected and raised high into the pale blue sky.

Then the crane began to lift the blades down and off the stem of the turbine. On the ground the blades and generator were dismantled from the hub and loaded onto one of the trucks. It rumbled off to the highway. Then the three sections of the stem were lifted off and lowered down at the rate of about one per hour. By four o'clock in the afternoon the last of the wind turbine was gone. All that was left was the gravel road and a concrete slab with a hole in it. Meg sat in her chair among her collectibles, a drink by her side, and watched the sun slowly set over the far shore of the lake. Her eye kept glancing to where she had watched the flashing red light atop the wind turbine blink on and off for over a year. It was hard to believe it was gone forever; like the man, whose name she would not allow herself to think of anymore.

Molly had spent her afternoon in the studio, having no interest in the dismantling of the wind turbine other than wondering how Meg was enjoying the show. Molly was too busy working on her novel, too obsessed with the daily groove of turning out ten pages per day. She had read *The Needle's Eye* and was heavily influenced by the style and form of that type of novel. Perhaps it was the Irish in her that led her to write in streaming free flowing prose. Then again, she thought, maybe it was the Muse that Roland had left in the cheese shed for her. She was writing like a mad woman, sending chapters to Harry Stompe, who was going to publish her.

When the kids got home there was the happy chatter of young school girls and their daily adventures. Molly did have to break down and get a TV for which she hoped Roland would forgive her. Despite the boob tube, the girls were doing great in school. Sony leaked that Melanie had a boyfriend and Melanie leaked that Sony had been yelled at by the bus driver. In actions and in words, Pipe was now home, like the other one had ever existed.

When Molly got word that Mrs. Dankermann had died two days later, she and the girls drove into town to Stanhope's for the wake. It was there that she ran into Meg Bollander. They both saw each other at the same time and looked away, but they kept catching each other's furtive glances. Molly thought it was time for the neighbors to have a talk.

"Meg, don't run away from me," said Molly as Meg started to turn her back.

Meg shrugged. She was busted. "Hello, Molly, nice to see you." The sentence dangled off without sincerity.

"You haven't been much of a neighbor, Meg. Why didn't you return my calls?

"Wouldn't be right, us being friendly."

"Why, for God's sake?"

Meg was getting flustered. She really didn't want this conversation, but now that it was right in front of her there was no hiding from it. "Because you're his daughter now." She looked around for help, but only saw Mrs. Dankermann looking slightly deader than the last time she saw her alive. "That's it, okay?"

"His daughter? His...he, Roland Heinz, just reached out from his grave two days ago and took down that wind turbine as a gesture to you! Jesus Christ, Meg, do you have any idea what that cost and how much wrangling that man had to do? "The..." Molly hushed her voice several levels. "The fucking Governor had to sign an order to get Alliant to take that thing down. That damned windmill is the only one in the country that had been taken off line because some old man wanted to make peace with some old woman."

Meg was speechless, still looking to the corpse for help.

"Oh, shit, you're never going to change are you?"

"It's unlikely."

"Well, too bad, Meg. The girls liked you. They could...I could use another friend around here and here you are clinging to some old grudge like it was sacred."

"I'm sorry, Molly. That's just the way I am."

Molly could only shake her head. She turned to locate the girls and started to walk away when Meg spoke up again.

"Molly."

"Yeah, what, is it, Meg?"

"I know I got no right, but I need to ask you something."

"Go ahead."

"Who the heck is or was Sorry Heinz? That's the only thing I really couldn't figure out."

Molly suddenly felt pity for Meg. She kept trying to be free of Roland, but something was always dragging her back in. She guessed this last bit of information would do little to ease her mind, but it might soothe her curiosity. She turned and leaned in close to Meg.

"Sorry was the dog he had for many years, Meg."

"The dog? You mean that stupid black and white collie or whatever it was?"

Molly was astounded to see something almost, but not quite a smile come across Meg's face.

"Yeah, that dog. Sorry was her name."

"Hah, I saw him and that dog wandering around his property. Wondered why he kept it."

"He kept it because he loved it, Meg."

"Yeah, he could love a dog, I suppose, but when I tied that dog to his tree over in Chilton I did it because I figured the infernal barking would drive him crazy. That dog never stopped barking. That's why I got rid of it. But, I guess I get it now. Goodbye, Molly Costello."

Meg exited out a side door of the funeral parlor leaving Molly stunned. She was trying hard to digest the fact that Sorry the dog, the living catalyst that inspired Roland Heinz to begin to write his beautiful books was in fact, a gift from the woman who hated him. And neither of them ever knew it. Melanie walked up just then.

"Mom, you look funny," Mel said.

"I just heard the neatest story ever, honey."

"What story?" asked Sony as she took her mom's hand.

"Well, ladies, once upon a time...," Molly began as the three women marched passed Mrs. Dankermann and headed outside and back to their Ghost Farm.

EPILOGUE

A man and a woman sat on a fallen tree trunk overlooking Lake Winnebago. It was late January and the pale, cold sun was nearly down to the far shore of the ice-covered expanse. The two people passed a flask of something warming, while steam bled from their noses like pipe smoke. They seemed to be enjoying each other's company, exchanging occasional nudges and rocking laughter. Neither one seemed to mind the cold, lost in a conversation that they alone could hear. The woods surrounding them were bare, but starkly beautiful, poetic, and complex.

Just before the sun slid below the horizon it shot a flaming orange light into the woods that lit the people's faces and drew their attention to the perfect round disc. In the time it took to take ten breaths the light changed to a salmon pink and the shadows began to lengthen behind them, rushing to the darkening eastern sky. Ten breaths later the color became an amethyst purple, the last shade before darkness and the most beautiful and royal. The man and woman watched the sun flatten and fade now as the Dog Star ascended. The couple stood then and began to walk away. The man put his arm around the woman as they walked and if you had been close enough you might have heard them whisper.

"We should go now. Go back. The show is over," the man said.

"You were right, it was truly a beautiful place to watch the day end," said the woman as she leaned into him. "But, it's time now to go a' haunting, right?"

"Yes, time for that."

"Do we haunt the house or the barn?"

"Hah, the house is already haunted by the old farmers and the barn is haunted by an owl."

"So where do we go a' haunting, Father?"

"We go where we belong, dear. Where we always belonged."

"And where is that?"

"Ah, my dearest Garnet, we haunt the pages of books."

And everywhere there were birds.

LaVergne, TN USA
08 February 2010
172491LV00001B/3/P